KU-015-221

Time to Kill

Ten years after the end of the Civil War, Nat Jordan who has fought in the Confederate army, is returning by railroad to his home near Kansas City.

Then they are held up by so-called Quantrill raiders, led by Captain Coulter with whom Jordan had escaped from Union forces during the war, Coulter recognizes Jordan and this soon leads to complications.

A Pinkerton agent called McGill suspects that Jordan is in cahoots with the raiders, and things begin to turn very nasty when tragedy strikes at the Jordan homestead.

Who is on the side of the raiders and who is on the side of the law? It is time to kill, but who will die?

By the same author

Shoot-out at Big King
Man of Blood
Riders From Hell

Time to Kill

Lee Lejeune

A Black Horse Western

ROBERT HALE · LONDON

© Lee Lejeune 2009
First published in Great Britain 2009

ISBN 978-0-7090-8739-7

Robert Hale Limited
Clerkenwell House
Clerkenwell Green
London EC1R 0HT

www.halebooks.com

The right of Lee Lejeune to be identified as
author of this work has been asserted by him
in accordance with the Copyright, Designs and
Patents Act 1988

MORAY COUNCIL LIBRARIES & INFO.SERVICES	
20 27 23 23	
Askews	
WF	

Typeset by
Derek Doyle & Associates, Shaw Heath
Printed and bound in Great Britain by
CPI Antony Rowe, Chippenham and Eastbourne

CHAPTER ONE

Nat Jordan was leaning against the window in the train headed for Kansas City . . . headed for home. That was the way he liked to think of it. Home was a homestead in Missouri but he hadn't seen it since he left to fight in the Confederate Army in '62. It was now the summer of '75 and the war had been over for ten years. At least that's what Nat Jordan figured.

Nat was a hardened warrior and he looked like it. Complexion of seasoned leather, eyes keen as an eagle's, lips and jaw taut and ready. A face that had seen a lot of action and a deal of horror and had come through, scarred but toughened, like a pair of boots that had seen much service.

'You travelling west, Soldier?' the man sitting opposite crowed in a voice that came from the East, probably from New York City or somewhere.

Nat Jordan focused his keen blue eyes on the stranger and gave him the once over. A small-boned guy wearing a new-style bowler hat at a jaunty angle; moustache flowing down to his jawbones; check tie matching a check suit; a fiddle laid out on his lap as though ready for tuning: some kind of wandering musician, or a confidence trickster, maybe.

'Train's going west,' Jordan agreed ironically. 'So I guess that's where I'm headed.' His voice was deep, some might have said mellifluous, but his tone was wary as if he was cautious about sharing his thoughts with a stranger.

The man with the fiddle wasn't easily put off. He let out a peal of laughter. 'Got me there!' he said. 'I'm Preacher Man, by the way. That's what they called me way back and that's what's stuck.'

Jordan eyed him over again. 'Don't look like a preacher,' he said. 'More like a wandering fiddler.'

Preacher Man grinned, showing one gold tooth prominent in the front of his mouth. 'Oh, I'm that too!' he boasted. 'Been most everything in my time. Preaching, fiddling, horse doctoring. I've done it all from California to Baltimore, even down to the Mexican border and back. Can't seem to get my roots down in the dirt and maybe I don't choose to, anyway.' He patted his fiddle hopefully. 'This here is my fiddle. Best friend I ever had. Scraping it got me out of many a tight corner. Ain't that so, old buddy?' He stroked and patted the fiddle like it was a favourite lover lying across his thigh. Then he turned his dancing eyes on Jordan again. 'My guess is I was right about you. You've been a fighting man.'

Though Jordan was wary of strangers, he gave a faint grin. He had to admit that Preacher Man had a good, open manner. A bedside way with horses as well as the fiddle, maybe. 'What fighting I've done is all in the past,' he said. 'A man gets tired of fighting and killing.'

'I guess that's why you're going home,' Preacher Man said. 'Swords into ploughshares, I suspect.'

'Something like that,' Jordan agreed.

That was where the conversation might have ended or gone on into new territory, but Jordan felt the locomotive starting to puff less steadily and it was losing power. He glanced out of the window and saw a string of riders galloping alongside. There could have been fifteen or twenty of them and they were keeping pace with the train. Two particular things he noticed about them: they were all armed and some of them wore bits and pieces of Confederate Army uniform despite the fact that the so-called Rebs had been defeated ten years before.

'Well, this doesn't look so good,' Preacher Man said, as the locomotive slowed and then came to a dragging halt. Several of the other passengers had got to their feet to peer out of the window.

'My God!' said one. 'It's them!'

'It's those Quantrills,' another horrified voice cried out.

'Sure looks like it!' Preacher Man said buoyantly. Seemed he didn't give a damn about the train being held up. Might even relish the excitement.

A woman screamed. 'Those desperate men steal and rape!' she gasped.

'You don't need to fret none about the raping bit, ma'am,' Preacher Man reassured her.

Now the locomotive had come to a stop, still puffing out its smoke like a giant glad to take a breather. Everyone in the carriage became frozen with a kind of horror of anticipation.

Nat Jordan watched from the window as the riders assembled round the caboose with their guns held high. Though he couldn't see everything from where he sat, he guessed from the shouting voices that some of them were coming on board.

Preacher Man leaned forward and muttered in a confidential tone, 'It's those Quantrills for sure.'

Jordan had heard about the Quantrill Raiders, named after Colonel William Clarke Quantrill, their founder. A band of guerrilla fighters who fought the war by other means, raiding and killing and looting in the name of the Confederate cause. For them pillage and killing was justification enough even after the war had ended. As he watched the bandits prancing and circling round the caboose, he noticed they weren't wearing masks or bandannas to cover their faces. That seemed like bare-faced brazenness, but it made him smile.

The connecting door was pushed open and a cabman entered, shaking and trying to appear calm. 'Please don't disturb yourselves, ladies and gentlemen. It seems we have a slight problem here. There's something blocking the line and we have to stop for a while.'

'Is there a hold-up?' a man in a seat close to Jordan blurted out.

'Well,' the cabman said, 'let's just say we have to pause a little.' He stood in the gangway fingering his watch chain and trying to look smug and reassuring but his eyes were darting around like panicky birds in the bushes.

Preacher Man raised his fiddle and looked as though he was about to play a jig but someone pushed the cabman aside and elbowed his way into the carriage. He was followed by two bearded *hombres* toting Winchesters.

'The cabman is right,' the man in the doorway said in a light-hearted manner. 'No need to get agitated, folks. Just so long as you hand over your valuables in a good cause.'

That created something of a flutter, especially among the ladies, and Preacher Man apparently had second thoughts about playing his fiddle. 'Excuse me, sir,' he piped up in a wheedling kind of voice. 'We're mostly poor folk going to visit brothers and sisters in Kansas City or there about. So we don't have much in the way of valuables.'

The leader of the bandits who wore a big black Stetson hat came along and looked down at Preacher Man. 'And who may you be, sir?'

Preacher Man showed his gold tooth and tipped his bowler hat. 'Just call me Preacher Man,' he said.

'Well, Preacher Man,' the man in the black Stetson said, 'you don't have to trouble yourself too much. I'm a modest man. I'd be happy to take a gold ring or two, a hunter watch, whatever you have to spare . . . all in the cause of charity.'

A woman close by gasped and fell forward in a faint. A bolder man described the situation as outrageous. The man in the black Stetson responded with a laugh. The two bearded *hombres* with Winchesters chuckled indulgently. One of them removed a top hat from the head of a sedate-looking gent who looked like a banker and started shaking it in the faces of the other passengers while the other bearded *hombre* pointed his Winchester at their heads.

'Just in the cause of charity,' one of them said.

'And you, sir,' – the man in the black Stetson was staring down at Jordan – 'what have you to put in our modest poor box?'

Nat Jordan was still staring out of the window. He turned slowly to regard the man. 'Not a thing,' he announced calmly. Anyone looking at him closely might have seen the muscles at the side of his jaws tighten and his eyes turned as cold as a mountain in a midwinter storm.

'Not a thing!' echoed the man.

'Not a thing, Mr Coulter,' Jordan said.

At the name *Coulter* brought out so clearly and strongly, the man stiffened and drew back. 'Who the hell are you?' he demanded.

Jordan looked at him calmly and grinned. 'Name's Jordan,' he pronounced slowly, 'Nat Jordan, and you're Captain Coulter of the late Confederate Army.'

Coulter looked at Jordan sharply and then with sudden recognition. 'Jordan,' he breathed. 'Nat Jordan, so it is.' An expression, something between pleasure and suspicion hovered on his lips. Preacher Man, watching closely, might have said he was disconcerted – possibly even a little embarrassed!

Then Preacher Man saw something even more surprising. Jordan reached inside his old fustian jacket and produced a gold fob watch. He held it up, pressed a button on its side and it chimed, not loudly, but clearly enough for all the passengers close by to hear. He raised it slightly, examined it closely, and returned it slickly to his inner pocket.

To Preacher Man's amazement, Captain Coulter merely laughed and waved his hand dismissively.

'Well, I'll be goldarned! So it's you, Jordan,' Coulter said, and passed on through the cab still chuckling quietly to himself.

'He'll be goldarned!' Preacher Man gasped. 'I'll be double goldarned!' He sat staring at Jordan with his mouth open. Jordan saw there was only the one gold tooth in the cavern of his jaw.

As the men with the Winchesters moved on through the car, the passengers began to stir in amazement: 'They stole my watch!' 'Those men took my diamond ear-rings!' 'They looked right through my purse and took my gold coins!'

The man who had been bold enough to describe the incident as *outrageous* stood up and glared at Jordan. 'What's the meaning of this? They took our valuables and terrified the women! Why didn't they take your gold watch?'

Jordan shrugged. 'Personal reasons, I guess,' he said drily.

The man came closer and breathed over Jordan with menace. 'You knew that robber. You called him Coulter – Captain Coulter.'

Jordan didn't deny it. 'Maybe I did,' he said, 'and maybe I didn't. What's that to you?'

The big red-faced man looked around at the other passengers for support. 'He didn't take your gold watch! You must in with those raiders.'

Jordan regarded him with the coolness of a lion regarding a man on the other side of the bars of its cage. 'I'm just a man going home to take my rest after the horrors of a long war,' he said.

'But that war's been over for ten years,' his accuser said.

'That's what they say,' Jordan agreed.

Preacher Man intervened. 'Seems those Quantrills haven't yet got wise to that fact.'

The red-jowled man was ready to push his luck a bit further. 'How come that man Coulter didn't take your watch?' he demanded.

'As I said, personal reasons,' Jordan replied. 'Anyway, I didn't offer it.'

There was a faint titter of nervous laughter from further down the car.

The red-faced man looked even angrier, but before he could say another word, there came shouts and the sound of shooting from the caboose area.

'My Gawd, now they're going to kill us all!' a woman shrieked.

Jordan turned his attention to the window again. He saw the raiders circling and whirling, their guns held high like something serious had occurred down there.

Everyone became quiet and tense with expectation in the carriage, fearful that something even more terrible was about to happen. People were looking at Jordan as though half afraid he intended to leap up and strangle his accuser.

Jordan was sitting still, considering matters. He had his knapsack on the seat beside him.

The Quantrill Raiders were turning and grouping, ready to ride away. As Jordan watched, Coulter appeared below. He was riding a handsome roan with a flowing mane. He turned in the saddle and gave Jordan a brisk cutaway salute. Then the whole bunch of riders rode away in a swirl of dust.

'They've gone,' someone gasped.

There was a hubbub of relief. Then a silence descended on the passengers. They seemed to crouch down in their seats as though half afraid the raiders would return.

11

For a moment nothing happened. Then the door of the carriage opened and the cabman reappeared. He had his hands clasped together over his fat belly as though trying to produce an air of calm, but his eyes were darting about even more like birds in a storm.

'Please stay in your seats, ladies and gentlemen. We hope to have the track cleared very shortly. And we can continue our journey to Kansas City. The company apologizes for the delay.'

'Delay, you say!' the outraged gentleman fumed. 'Those bandits held us up and stole our valuables. That's a deal more than an unfortunate delay!'

'And we heard shooting too!' a woman cried. 'Did someone get hurt?'

The cabman looked even more apologetic. Though he strove to keep his dignity, he was obviously close to tears. 'Someone got shot, ma'am,' he said.

'Someone got shot!' the woman gasped. 'Who was it got shot?' She was standing in the gangway, her face as yellow as curd.

'Please keep calm, ma'am,' the cabman pleaded. 'They got the guard.'

'Is there a doctor on board?' someone shouted. 'He'll need a doctor!'

'Too late for that,' the cabman croaked. He indicated a point in the middle of his forehead. 'They got him right here between the eyes.'

The guard, it seemed, had reached for a shotgun he had hidden in the cab, but before he could use it, one of the raiders had shot him clean through the head.

A woman screamed. 'My Gawd, those desperate men might come back and rape and kill us all.'

'As I said, you don't need to worry on either score, ma'am,' Preacher Man said. 'They just rode off. We can still see the dust where they hightailed it.'

12

'Took our valuables too,' the man with the top hat complained.

The cabman raised his hands. 'This is all very worrying, folks, but I assure you we'll be on our way just as soon as they've cleared the track.'

Preacher Man raised his fiddle. 'Maybe I should play a few notes of sympathy for the good guard.' Before anyone could protest he tucked his fiddle under his chin and started to play. To everyone's surprise, the tune came out sweet and sad, and soon most of the passengers had settled down into a horrified silence.

The train got up steam again and started forward with a lurch.

Preacher Man laid his fiddle on his knees. He leaned forward confidentially to Jordan. 'How come you didn't take a shot at that man Coulter?' he asked.

Jordan stared back at him without surprise. 'Why should I do that, Mr Preacher Man?'

Preacher Man gestured towards the knapsack sitting on the seat next to Jordan. 'You got a shooter in that knapsack beside you. Why didn't you draw it out and shoot that man?'

Jordan still showed no flicker of surprise, though Preacher Man was right. In a pocket of his knapsack he had a brand new Colt .45 with six rounds in it. How could Preacher Man know that?

'There's one man killed,' Jordan said. 'Did you want a blood bath in here?'

Preacher Man nodded with quiet satisfaction. 'Those men toting Winchesters would have caused a massacre,' he agreed. 'I guess you seen enough killing in your time, Soldier.'

Jordan nodded grimly. 'More than enough for one life,' he agreed.

Preacher Man leaned a little closer. 'Another thing, how come you knew that man Coulter?'

13

Jordan sat back in his seat and remembered the past.

The platoon had broken away from the battle. It now lay crumpled and bloody like a sodden pack of cards scattered in a creek. One minute it had been a disciplined fighting unit pouring hot lead into the enemy. Next, there was a weird unearthly cry and the ranks broke like a holed dyke and crumbled away into the creek. Before Sergeant Ballard could bellow out an order to steady the troop, men were floundering in the surging torrent, clawing their way in disarray and panic to the opposite bank, trying desperately to save themselves.

Jordan was still in position, firing at the shadowy forms of the advancing enemy. It's kill or be killed, he thought, as the man on his left turned and plunged into the river. But the fleeing man never had the chance to swim or wade. A fist seemed to punch out of the gloom and take half his head away. He took two steps and flopped face forward, dead before he hit the water.

'Keep your goddamn head down!' Jordan muttered to himself. 'And for God's sake don't panic!'

He wasn't about to risk having his head blown off. Everything seemed to be happening in a confused dream. He could see the crouching terrified figures of the advancing Union Army and knew if he stayed long enough one of them would skewer him with a sword or blow his brains out like the man in the river!

Was he on his own? Close beside him crouched another figure. Not a dead man sliding down the bank, but Captain Coulter himself.

'Those damned cowardly bastards!' Coulter muttered. He had a pistol in each hand and, as the shadowy figure of a Union soldier reared up before him, he took a snap shot into its face. The man jerked and plunged down beside him

14

and slid on into the crimsoning water.

'We got to get out of here!' the captain said. He glanced sideways and waved a pistol. 'You slide along to that jetty. I'll give you cover and then follow. You can cover me from the jetty!'

Maybe it wasn't a good plan, but it was the only plan. Without questioning it, Jordan ducked down below the bank and waded as fast as he could towards the jetty. When he reached it, he saw it provided some cover. He crouched down behind it and started to fire at the Union soldiers who were already beginning to run out of steam. Coulter's fire had been steady and withering; he knew how to hold his fire until he saw the whites of their eyes.

Now Coulter ducked down close to the bank and followed Jordan to the jetty. A Union soldier reared up behind him ready to take a shot. Jordan steadied his arm and took a blast. The man reared back and slid down on the bank like he was about to take a nap.

Coulter came wading, following the line of the bank.

'Thanks, Soldier!' Coulter breathed through his teeth.

Tethered to the jetty were the remains of a battered boat, still afloat, enough to give them cover against the advancing army. Without pausing to discuss matters, they cut it adrift and started to propel it across the creek, ducking behind it for cover.

Spouts of water sprang up all round them as they pushed it across to the opposite bank.

On the other side, Jordan put out his hand, grasped the captain by the shoulder of his jacket and hauled him onto the bank.

A hundred yards to their left the blue-bellies were breaking through, swarming over the bank and wading across the creek with their weapons held high. Because the Rebs were in flight they were roaring in triumph.

'Punch drunk,' Captain Coulter muttered. 'Do we sit here and wait for the Grim Reaper or make for the barn?'

The barn seemed to be a good idea. It had been Company HQ just a week before. A good place, maybe, to recover their wind. There was dead ground between them and the advancing Yankees. So they ducked and ran for the dilapidated building.

The barn was dark and smelled of burned wood and hay. Jordan and Captain Coulter threw themselves inside and lay for a moment, getting their breath back. But not for long. Coulter started checking his weapons to make sure they were dry and loaded.

Jordan heard groans and suppressed breathing. He swung round with his weapon ready to see two figures sprawled out on the straw. One man had blood on his shoulder and chest. The other seemed just plumb shit scared.

'Don't shoot!' the man pleaded.

'We're Confederate,' Jordan said. 'Keep quiet. Those Yankees might pass us by.'

Not likely, he thought.

Coulter was peering through a crack in the side of the barn. 'Here they come,' he warned.

Jordan looked out and saw a handful of Yankee soldiers picking their way cautiously towards the barn – not more than ten of them. Maybe we could take them out! he thought.

Coulter had had the same idea. He had found a kind of loophole high up with a fairly good line of fire. Before Jordan could say, I don't think you should do that, he had pumped out two shots at the advancing soldiers. One flung up his weapon and pitched over on his side. The other had been lifted off the ground and thrown onto his back. The rest of the bunch fell down on their faces behind whatever cover they could find.

That was a brave damned fool thing to do, Jordan thought, specially as it will soon be sundown. Apparently the enemy were well disciplined. Jordan could hear a sergeant, or whoever was in command, barking out orders. He looked out through a crack and saw that the soldiers out there had all ducked down and were well hidden.

Seconds went by. The man with the ball in his shoulder groaned. The other man was trying to get up but he was too shaky with fear to control his legs. 'They're going to kill us,' he cried.

'Keep your damned shit to yourself!' Coulter growled from above. 'You make any more moaning, I kill you myself.'

A voice came from outside. 'You men in there. We got you trapped. You come out with your hands held high, you get to live. You stay holed up in there, you die. That's no never-mind to us out here.' The voice came out cheerful but strong.

The man with the shaky legs was crawling towards the door. 'I'm going to go out there and give myself up,' he said.

Coulter turned with a gun on the man. 'You touch that door, you're a dead man!' he said. The man with shaky legs whose knees were beginning to go collapsed against the side of the barn. 'You wouldn't shoot one of your own men, Captain.'

Coulter cocked his pistol. 'I'd kill a coward as good as killing a rat,' he threatened.

Jordan knew he meant it, but he didn't have time to say so because there was a movement outside the door and he knew the Union men had crept up outside and were piling things against the door to keep them blocked up inside. That sergeant is pretty determined, he thought. He suddenly knew they meant to smoke them out.

'Come out while you still got the chance!' the sergeant shouted.

'They got us like rats in a trap!' the terrified man whimpered. The man with the hole in his shoulder groaned. He wasn't going anywhere.

'We're gonna burn!' the soldier with the shaky legs cried out.

You're damned right! Jordan thought.

One of the Yankees had crept up and hurled a flaming torch up onto the broken roof. Flame and sparks hurled down onto the floor below. It was a tinder-box: they had no way of staunching the flames!

Coulter slid down from his vantage point and looked around. 'We got to get out of here,' he said, 'if we don't want to fry!'

Jordan was way ahead of him. He was searching around at the back of the barn where he remembered seeing a long handled axe a week earlier. He found it like a charm.

The flames were already taking hold. Nobody in that barn was likely to survive more than a minute. Jordan swung the axe at the back end of the barn and broken timbers started to split, just enough to let a man squeeze through.

The man with the hole in his shoulder was beginning to retch and cough with the smoke. The soldier with the shaky legs was screaming and struggling to claw his way, first to the blocked door and then towards the gap Jordan had made in the opposite wall.

He gets in that hole, shouting and screaming, Jordan thought, we're all dead meat! as he swung the axe to widen the gap.

'Don't leave me!' the wounded man cried. He was struggling to get to his feet, but you could see he wasn't going to make it.

'Say your prayers,' Coulter said, and shot him right through the head. The man jumped back like he'd been struck by the axe and fell sideways with blood spurting from his head.

The other soldier was about to stick his head out through the gap Jordan had made with the axe but Coulter seized him by the belt and jerked him back and shot him through the side of the head. The impact of the bullet hurled him to one side where he lay kicking and jerking for a second, and then gasped out his last breath.

'Get through! Get through!' Coulter said, close to Jordan's ear.

Jordan was already halfway through the opening. He knew it was his only chance. The barn was a roaring inferno and Coulter had a gun on him. He slithered out onto the wet grass and crawled away from the flaming barn as fast as he could. He knew they had the place surrounded and expected the impact of a bullet every second.

Coulter flopped down beside him and they both breathed like engines for a moment.

'We got to go!' Coulter said hoarsely. 'We got to run for that stand of trees over there. Only chance.'

As he got up on his knees, the figure of a soldier reared up before him, spurting flame.

Jordan crouched, held his breath, and pumped off a round. The soldier jerked and fell.

The two Confederates ran, swerving and weaving towards the trees. The Yankees fired a couple rounds at them but already it was getting dark, except for the yellow roaring flames of the flaming barn.

That Captain Coulter's got balls! Jordan conceded, as they gained the cover of the trees.

19

CHAPTER TWO

Kansas City had changed considerably since Jordan was last there. Bigger, of course, and more bustling. When he got off the train he was accosted by a rail track official in an impressive blue uniform. He looked like an admiral or a naval captain at least.

'Mind if I ask, did you see the shooting?' the man enquired. He was holding a notebook and pencil.

'Saw the train robbers, heard the shooting,' Jordan responded.

'We shall need witnesses,' the man said. 'Do you plan to stay in town?'

'A few days maybe,' Jordan conceded.

'May I enquire where you might be lodging?' the official said.

'The Blue Star,' Preacher Man responded.

The official wrote this down in a notebook and the two passed on.

'What's with The Blue Star?' Jordan asked. 'How come I'm staying at The Blue Star? You got an interest in the establishment?'

Preacher Man now had his fiddle in its case and a carpet-bag over his shoulder. Jordan, a good head taller, had his knapsack on his back and his soldier's cap on his head.

Preacher Man confided, 'You look like a stranger from a

foreign land. There's always someone ready to take advantage of a stranger in this town.' He nodded and grinned amiably. 'I think you'll like The Blue Star. Not too expensive, not too cheap. Manager's an old buddy of mine. Name of Ringo. He'll give you a good deal.'

Jordan decided to go along with the notion. Preacher Man kind of fascinated him and The Blue Star was only a step from the railroad station.

They gave Jordan a room at the top of the house where he could look out and see the scurrying crowds beneath. As soon as he had thrown his knapsack down on the bed and tested the springs, he looked out between the curtains and saw a guy standing on the sidewalk, a city type smoking a big cigar and looking the The Blue Star over. That was no big deal, but Jordan had a sudden hunch similar to those in the war when the Yankees were about to launch a big attack. It was like in a play when the director wanted to focus attention on a particular character. So he'll tell the actor to keep perfectly still while everyone else milled around. That's the way the man with the big cigar looked. And he played along in character too.

He looked up and squinted along the line of windows in The Blue Star as if he was searching for someone.

Jordan reached into his knapsack and yanked out the Peacemaker Colt with its cartridge belt and holster. He eased the revolver out of its holster and held it close to his nostrils and smelt oil and shot. He had fired the piece a number of times but so far not in anger.

He slid the revolver back into its holster and went downstairs for dinner and found Preacher Man already seated at a table. He had his fiddle in its case beside him and he motioned Jordan over to the table. Jordan was by way of being a loner, so he paused until Madame Marina came over to him.

21

'Ah, Mr Jordan, I hope your room is OK. We have reserved a place for you at Mr Preacher Man's table. He's expecting you.'

Jordan followed her over to the table and she handed him a menu. He nodded to Preacher Man and sat down opposite him.

'You my fairy godmother or something?' he asked.

Preacher Man was shaking with silent laughter. 'Like I said, there are a lot of undesirable elements in this town, and I thought you'd appreciate the company. I should take the beef. They do it good here.'

When Madame Marina came back, Jordan ordered the beef though he was tempted to try something else to show his independence.

'Good choice,' Preacher Man said with twinkling eyes. 'There'll be music and dancing girls later. And I guess Marina and Ringo will ask me to play a few notes on my fiddle. They like to dance here.'

The food arrived and Jordan thought it looked nice and tasty.

'Too bad about the guard,' Preacher Man said. 'They say he was a good family man, but he shouldn't have pulled a gun on those Quantrill Raiders.'

Jordan hardly paused in his eating. 'Colonel William Quantrill died back in '65,' he said.

'So you say,' Preacher Man rejoined, 'and so you may believe. But I hear different.'

Jordan grinned. 'What different?'

Preacher Man laid aside the fork with which he had been spiking his beef. 'Some say he's down Texas way teaching school. All that dying talk is so much hogwash put out by politicians. That's what they say.'

Jordan shrugged. 'Old soldiers never die. That's another saying.'

Preacher Man leaned forward with interest. Tell me about Coulter?' he asked, in little more than a whisper.

Jordan was still grinning but his grin held the suggestion of suspicion. 'Who wants to know?' he said.

'I want to know,' Preacher Man said. 'And I'm not the only one. He could have shot us all on the train. A man's entitled to know who intends to shoot him.'

Jordan went on chewing his beef for a while. 'I guess that's why you put on the fairy godmother act?' he asked drily.

'Now, now,' Preacher Man chided, 'you surely don't believe that. A man sits opposite a stranger on a train. Can't he be civil?'

Jordan raised his eyebrows. 'Could be a lot of reasons for being civil.'

Preacher Man chuckled. 'I guess there might be a sizeable price on that man Coulter's head. Did you think of that?'

'Didn't cross my mind,' Jordan said wryly.

Before Preacher Man could respond, the three musicians who constituted a band struck up close by on what served as a stage. The curtains jerked open by degrees, and half-a-dozen highly made-up females started dancing the can-can.

'Ain't those girls just beautiful?' Preacher Man said with appreciation.

Jordan couldn't make up his mind to agree. The *girls* of uncertain age wore crimson dresses, cut away to expose their twinkling legs and their make-up was so lavishly applied it looked like they were wearing Chinese masks. Nevertheless, roars of appreciation and clouds of approving smoke rose from all quarters of the audience.

Marina appeared at their table. 'I hope you gentlemen enjoyed your food?' she said, batting her eyelids at Jordan.

'That beef was something else again,' Preacher Man said.

He ordered two more beers for the table. 'Could have rye,' he confided to Jordan, 'but I got to keep a steady head for my performance.'

When the girls stopped kicking their legs up and the band retired for well-earned refreshments, Marina's husband, Ringo, got up on the stage and announced an unexpected treat: the great fiddle player *Alonso* would now grace the company with a few well-known melodies.

To Jordan's surprise, Preacher Man rose and bowed and made his way to the stage. Not for the first time, Jordan thought, as the fiddle began to scrape away. Preacher Man was certainly a fiddler of some accomplishment and he went through his selection at a roaring pace.

Then Jordan glanced to one side and saw a man smoking a big cigar standing beside his table. He was big with a wide belly, across which stretched a gold watch chain. He was wearing a sombre-looking bowler. Just below his fancy waist-coat he wore a broad belt and, under the flap of his dark jacket, Jordan suspected, he had a hidden revolver.

'Excuse me,' the man said genially. 'May I ask you to spare a moment of your time?'

Jordan gave him a level, calculating look. 'Business or pleasure?' he asked.

The man raised his bushy eyebrows and grinned. 'Could be either, or both,' he said. 'I'm McGill. I believe you're Nat Jordan?'

Jordan drank his beer and considered matters. This was the man who had surveyed The Blue Star from the opposite sidewalk. 'Let's stick to business,' he said.

McGill nodded. He drew out a chair and sat down opposite Jordan.

'Have a cigar,' he said. 'These are good Havanas.'

'Thanks. I don't smoke after dinner.'

McGill inclined his head. He drew out a pocket book and

24

flicked a card across the table. 'I represent the Pinkerton Detective Agency. I believe you were travelling on the train from the East, the one that was held up.' He leaned forward earnestly. 'The guard was shot dead by the hold-up men.'

Jordan nodded and held his gaze. 'Pity about that guard. They say he had a family. Maybe he shouldn't have gone for his gun.'

McGill inclined his head again. 'Somebody on board reported you spoke to the leader of that gang, man by the name of Coulter. Would that be right?'

Jordan considered the matter further. 'I knew Coulter back in the war,' he agreed. 'We faced some rough times together.'

McGill was smiling, a strange smile of agreement and complicity. 'You heard about the Quantrill Raiders, no doubt?'

Jordan nodded slowly. 'I know about the raiders.'

McGill was getting into his stride. 'Those Quantrills did a deal of killing and raping and burning supposedly for the Confederate cause.'

'So I heard.'

McGill shrugged. 'Quantrill himself was killed at the end of the war.'

'I heard that too.'

'But there are those who can't accept that the war is over, and those bandits still believe they have to rape and pillage for the Confederate cause.' He paused and lowered his voice. 'And that man Coulter is one of their leaders.'

Jordan took another sip of his beer. 'I hear what you say and I believe you,' he said.

McGill looked at the end of his cigar and shook the ash onto the tablecloth. 'I know you fought in the Confederate cause,' he said darkly. 'I believe you fought bravely and I know you got your pardon after the war.'

'I came out of that war with my life,' Jordan conceded. 'Why don't you spit out on the business and say what's on your mind?'

McGill gave a small sigh and nodded again. 'OK,' he said. 'I'll lay my cards right on the table. You know Coulter and Coulter knows you. You've been East since the war and now, after ten years, you choose to come West again. How come that is so?'

Jordan kept silent for a moment. He could see what the Pinkerton man was driving at. 'I had my reasons,' he said. 'Mostly family.'

'Reasons like you thought you might join those Quantrill rebels?' McGill put in grittily.

'Like I said, reasons, like family reasons,' Jordan countered.

McGill shrugged. 'Let me tell you something, Mr Jordan. There are some men who would find it hard to believe that.'

Jordan made no reply. He took McGill's point and he didn't like what he took.

McGill picked up the card he had flicked across the table and held it up. 'I understand what old comrades mean,' he said. 'I myself fought with the Union and I still think of those friends who died, many of them no more than boys.' He waved the card to and fro. 'We catch those killers dead or alive there could be a big reward,' he said. 'If you want to work with me, just get in touch. You'll find the Pinkerton address here below, on the card.' He dropped the card on the table and stood up.

'Remember one thing,' he added, 'those men are not soldiers any more; they're cold-blooded killers, like mad dogs with rabies. They've got to be sought out and killed.'

McGill nodded abruptly and turned. He threaded his way between the tables and disappeared.

Preacher Man's performance had finished with dancing

and a whirling of men and women. Those in the audience were roaring their applause and throwing up their hats and casting their small change onto the stage.

Preacher Man or *Alonso* sure was a popular fellow!

Jordan's mind went back to the beginning of the war that had torn the nation apart. Right back to the homestead close to the Kansas border. His father, Nathaniel Jordan, was like an old-time patriarch with a flowing white beard and intense blazing eyes who had trapped game and fought against the Indians with Jim Bridger and Jim Baker and had settled for a life of farming on the prairies further east. Married a girl called Mary Smith and raised a family, three girls and two boys. The older of the two boys was Nat Jordan.

All the Jordan kids worked like donkeys to make that farm successful. Nothing was wasted and everything was put to good use, until dark war clouds loomed on the horizon and young Nat started arguing matters out with his father.

Nobody argued with Nathaniel Jordan unless they wanted to feel his strap around their buttocks. Father was the boss man and nobody debated the point. That was until young Nat took the bullet between his teeth.

'You were always a restless kid,' Nat's mother warned him. 'Never learned to rein in your temper and button your lip.'

Nat still heard his mother's mellow voice in the small hours of the morning when he was far from sleep. He remembered it too when the fighting raged around him and fatally wounded men were crying out for their mothers as they died.

It all started simply enough. Old man Jordan was as firm as a rock on the Unionist cause when Kansas was Unionist and Missouri wavered between the Confederates and the

Unionists. You might have expected the old man to be a Confederate and his son to be Unionist, but in this family it worked the other way round. It wasn't a matter of slavery and anti-slavery, more a matter of generational difference. Young Nat chose the Confederates not because he favoured slavery but because he couldn't stop arguing with his father. And he didn't like the Northern culture. Nathaniel the elder came down on the side of the Union because he resented the power of the rich slave owners and wanted it broken. He also had a deep admiration for Abraham Lincoln, who was born in a log cabin and who pulled himself up by his bootstraps to become President.

The final row was deeply imprinted on Nat Jordan's mind.

'You leave this house, you don't come back!' the old man raved, his beard forking and flaring like he was a mad demon from hell.

'If I leave this damned house, I don't mean to come back!' young Nat retorted.

That was how Nat Jordan joined the Confederate Army.

'Well, what do you think of it?' Preacher Man asked, as he resumed his seat at the table.

'You can certainly play that fiddle,' Jordan said.

'He sure can,' Ringo agreed, as Marina his wife placed tall glasses of foaming beer on the table before them.

Preacher Man raised his glass and drank deeply. He winked at Jordan. 'You want for me to fix for one of those dancing girls to visit with you?'

Jordan grinned and thought of the mask-like harpies prancing on the stage. 'I don't think so,' he said. 'I may be a little tired but I'm not quite ready for death.'

Preacher Man nodded and twisted his moustache in a grin. 'Maybe later,' he said. He leaned forward. 'Saw you talking to your fat friend while I was playing.'

'No particular friend,' Jordan said. 'Just a nosy man who wanted to ask a few questions.'

Preacher Man was watching him closely. He's no slouch, Jordan thought.

'Guess you shouldn't have greeted that hold-up man by name,' he said. 'That throws a deal of suspicion on you. You know that?'

'Thanks for the tip,' Jordan said. 'I'll bear it in mind.'

He left the table and went up the creaking stairs to bed. He didn't know what to make of Preacher Man. One way or another, he was pretty smart, but he could be the kind of man to tail a man and pretend to be his friend when all he wanted was to dish him dirt.

When he unlocked the door of his room he knew at once that someone else had been in there. The faint scent of perfume hung in the air. He stood and wondered for a moment. Then it registered. When Marina bent over to give him his drink, he had caught it: the smell of her perfume.

He went to the window and dragged it open. There was plenty of roistering in the street below but no sign of the man Preacher Man had called 'his fat friend'.

His knapsack was still on the bed. He slid his hand inside and searched for the Colt. It was there all right, but had it been shifted to one aside?

I'm getting a little twitchy, he thought. But he could still catch the faint smell of cheap scent in the air.

CHAPTER THREE

Come morning the world looked a deal brighter to Jordan. Outside the roosters were crowing and he could hear the voices of men and woman going about their business.

He went down to the big room with the stage. A faint haze of stale tobacco smoke hung in the air and a man lay slumped over a table with his hat over his face like he had been there all night. Seated at another table with his back to the wall was Preacher Man. He looked quite sprightly after the night's incursions though now he didn't have his fiddle at his side.

He raised his hand cheerfully, and called out, 'Hi, pardner!'

Despite the brightness of a new day, Jordan didn't reply. Why is this little fiddle-player bugging me, he wondered? Has he some kind of con trick up his floppy sleeve?

'Come and join me for ham and eggs!' Preacher Man crowed.

Jordan saw that a place was already set for him. So he went across and sat down.

Preacher Man put his finger to his lips and gave a wink. 'Best to keep our voices down here,' he whispered. 'Never know who might be listening, do we?'

Jordan glanced around. All he could see was Ringo behind the bar and the man dressed in black apparently tight asleep with his head down and covered with a floppy hat on a neighbouring table.

'See you got yourself tooled up,' Preacher Man said. Jordan had strapped on his gunbelt which held the Peacemaker snug at his side. 'A wise precaution, ask me," Preacher Man added.

Jordan grunted. After the incidents of the day before, he thought it was best to be ready for any eventuality in this town.

Ringo brought him ham and eggs which looked inviting. 'You aim to stay another night?' he asked brightly.

Jordan exchanged glances with Preacher Man and Preacher Man signalled with his hand to keep his voice down. 'Guess I need to be moving on,' Jordan said.

Preacher Man put a brake on his tongue until Ringo had disappeared behind the counter again. 'You moving on, you're going to need a good piece of horse flesh under you,' he said.

Jordan was way ahead of him on that one.

'I could help you there,' Preacher Man offered. 'I know a man who'd give you a good deal, friend of mine, half Cherokee. He knows his horses and, as I think I told you, I have been a horse doctor of some distinction in my day. You're gonna need a horse and saddle, by my reckoning unless you mean to ride Injun style.'

Jordan thought about telling him to mind his own danged business, but now he had heard Preacher Man play the fiddle, his opinion of him had gone up considerably.

'Just down the road a piece,' Preacher Man said. 'Take less than five minutes to stroll there.'

They went over to the bar and checked out. As Ringo was writing his receipt Jordan caught Preacher Man's eye and he twitched his head sideways towards the man sleeping at the table close to the stage. The man had his eyes tight shut, still half concealed by his hat, and he looked as though he was about to slide out of his chair and onto the floor.

'We get all sorts around here,' Ringo said with a grin.

'Been here since last night, I guess,' Preacher Man said. 'Sleeping it off.'

Ringo held his head on one side. 'Not exactly,' he grinned. 'Came in a little before you this morning. Ordered a drink of rye. Obviously can't take his liquor.'

Jordan went upstairs to retrieve his knapsack and, when he came down, Preacher Man was still in conversation with Ringo. He had his carpet-bag and his fiddle and he was ready to go.

'You notice something?' Preacher Man said, when they were out on the sidewalk.

Jordan nodded. 'I noticed one thing,' he said. 'When I came down with my knapsack that bum sleeping close to the stage had lit out.'

'He crept out real quiet,' Preacher Man said. 'While I was passing the time of day with Ringo, the guy just took a powder and stole away. One minute he seemed to be snoozing like the dead; next minute he was gone like some kind of fairy in a fairy-tale.'

Jordan stood on the sidewalk glancing around. There was no sign of the sleeping man.

'You know what it means, don't you?' Preacher Man said.

'Could mean someone's taking a particular interest in our movements.'

'Could mean those friends of yours are keeping an eye on you.'

Jordan nodded. He thought it could be McGill or one of his buddies. Or it could be one of Coulter's sidekicks. Could be both are watching to see which way I jump. Not a comfortable thought.

They went into a store and Jordan bought himself a

brand new Stetson. Dark greeny-brown shade.

'That's a real nice headpiece,' Preacher Man said. 'Gives you the appearance of a real smart gent.'

If I'm going home I have to look kind of hand-in-hat, Jordan thought.

A few minutes later they were being greeted by Preacher Man's horse-dealing *compañero*, a man called Joe Jingalong. After the greeting between him and Preacher Man which involved much back slapping and hugging, Joe turned to Jordan and gave him a keen appraising look. 'You looking for good horse, mister?'

'We both need horses, I guess,' Preacher Man said. 'My friend needs a good strong riding horse. I need something a little smaller. Maybe a burro would do.'

Joe gave a high squeak of laughter. 'You don't need no burro, man. You need a good strong horse. I got plenty. Just come up from a breeding ranch I use. All good, well-bred horses.'

He led them out to the corral and Preacher Man roamed among the horses, examining them for canker wounds and running his hand over their backs to check their conformation, making sure they weren't cold jawed and camp-stallers. Jordan could see he was no phoney, that he had been a horse doctor of some distinction early on in life.

'This one's a good boy,' he advised, singling out a horse. 'He's no Sunday hoss.'

The horse he had chosen was tall at the shoulder and black with a white blaze down its nose; it had good strong legs and bright unflinching eyes. It had obviously been treated well.

'This is very good horse,' Joe Jingalong said. 'You can always tell a horse by its eye.'

They bargained for a bit until Jordan settled on a price he could afford. Always be ready to pay a little more for a

good horse, he reasoned. He could save you from an igno-
ble death in an emergency. So he paid a fair price for the
horse called Regius. Regius means king, and that's good
enough for me, he reasoned.

Preacher Man spent an equal amount of time choosing
his own mount which was a slightly shorter bay called
Monty. Monty had a good friendly eye, too.

'You travelling far?' Joe asked him.

Preacher was already saddling up Monty. 'Who knows?'
he shrugged. 'Depends where I'm blown, like the tumble-
weed.'

Preacher Man and Jordan paid their dues and mounted
up.

'May the Lord go with you,' Preacher Man said.

'Amen to that.' Jordan reached across and shook his
hand.

Was this the end of a perfect friendship?

Jordan rode out through the town, intending to strike
out for Redsville close by where his family homestead was
situated. Ten years is a long time and he felt wary, appre-
hensive about the way he might be received. Were his brothers and sisters still around? Was his dad still alive and fulmi-
nating about the Rebs? Would he be welcomed like the
prodigal son? Should he arrive at the house bearing gifts?
How could he account for the ten long years or more away
from the place?

As he rode down Main Street in Kansas City, he saw many
people driving buckboards and stopping at the stores to buy
provisions. It was clear the area had taken an upturn since
that ravaging war.

Or had it? With the so-called Quantrill raiders holding
up trains in the name of the defeated South, there was obviously still a deal of bitterness around. As he reflected on

this, a face loomed up like a phantom from the past: a woman around twenty-five or so hefting a big bag of provisions on a buckboard while the driver, a 'breed in his fifties sat in the driver's seat minding his own business and smoking a black cigarito.

Jordan swung down from his new mount and caught the bag of provisions as it was about to fall. 'Steady there, ma'am!'

The woman looked at him with a smile and then did a double take. She turned pale and stepped back as though she had seen some kind of apparition. 'Oh, my God!' she gasped.

Jordan knew he was no beauty with his weather-beaten features and his wry expression. Maybe it's the new Stetson, he thought.

He looked again and immediately recognized the face. 'Well I'll be damned,' he muttered. 'You're Beth Armitage!'

'The very same,' she breathed. 'And you're Nat Jordan unless you're a ghost.'

'No ghost,' he grinned. 'Not unless they didn't tell me yet.'

Beth Armitage was aghast. 'But they told me you were dead, killed in the war. That's why you never came back. That's what they said.'

That gave him a twinge of something like conscience. That must be what his folks must think. Beth Armitage came from a neighbouring outfit. When he left for the war she was nothing but a raw, bright-eyed kid. Now she was a full-grown woman with a strikingly attractive face and a freshness in her grey-blue eyes. He noted, however, that her dress was somewhat shabby, though she held herself with dignity.

'But I did come back,' he said. 'That's why I'm here.'

35

Beth Armitage reached out tentatively as if to verify her senses, and then thought better of it. 'Well,' she said somewhat formally, 'it's good to see you strong and well. I guess your folks will be glad to see you—'

'—Especially since they think I'm pushing up daisies somewhere East,' he prompted.

Beth hesitated over that, and he guessed he might have given her offence. 'None of my business,' she said, 'but it was a pity you had to quarrel with your pa so bitterly. But that's what that terrible war did to us, putting son against father, father against son.'

Jordan nodded. 'That is so,' he agreed. He remembered a story he had once read, how a son had to shoot his own father to stop him betraying the fact his regiment was camped in a gorge below. 'How is the old man?' he asked.

Beth bit her lip. 'I don't like to tell you this but your dad has got more political and even more patriotic since you went away. He's very bitter about the Confederates and even stronger on the Unionist cause than he was. I believe I heard he addressed a rally as recently as the other night. I know it worries your mother.'

Jordan felt the old storm clouds gathering in him again.

'As I recall, you went off to fight for the Rebs,' she added quietly.

Jordan nodded. 'That's over now,' he said. 'One gets plumb tired of killing.'

Beth's eyes went to the gunbelt but, instead of referring to it directly, she glanced over her shoulder at the 'breed smoking his cigarito. 'I heard about the train hold-up,' she murmured. 'How they killed the guard. That's simply terrible.'

Jordan admitted he was on the train but said nothing about meeting Coulter.

'All for nothing,' she added sadly. 'Those men are filled

36

with bitterness and hate. They've wreaked a deal of havoc in Missouri and Kansas.'

Jordan helped her up on the seat beside the 'breed. 'You on your way home?' he said.

'Family will be waiting for supplies,' she said. 'Usually manage with Redsville but here they do more and sometimes it's cheaper.'

'Maybe I could ride along shotgun,' Jordan suggested with a grin.

Beth looked down at the peacemaker at his side. 'I don't like those things, but you're welcome to ride along anyway.'

Jordan glanced at the 'breed and he grinned and gave him what looked like a wink.

So Jordan took his place beside the buckboard and they pulled away in the direction of Redsville.

As they rode along, Jordan was conscious of three things. First, he was going home; second, Beth Armitage had grown from a lanky, bright-eyed girl to a fine but modest woman; third, someone was tailing them.

He had conflicting feelings about going home. Beth Armitage's reaction to his sudden appearance had given him a flash of insight. What would his wild old father make of his coming? More important, what would his mother think? How would she react? And what about his brother and sisters, his sister Cary in particular, the one who had been closest to him. Maybe she and the others were married and away from home. And his brother Rick, how would he react to his brother's return after so many years?

'How's my brother Rick?' he asked. 'Is he doing good?'

Beth pulled a wry face. 'Rick went off like you, California or some place, looking for gold.'

'Is that right?' he marvelled. His brother had always been

mild as sheep cheese. 'Did he rile up the old man, too?'

Beth tossed her head. 'He just left to find his fortune, so I believe.'

Then Jordan turned his mind to the present certainty, that they were being tailed. In offering to ride shotgun even as a joke, he might have brought suspicion and danger on Beth and her cigarito-smoking driver.

When they were well on towards Redsville, he made his decision. They were driving through a stand of junipers when he peeled off and urged Regius to the right. 'Catch you later,' he said to Beth. Her driver glanced at him swiftly and drove on.

He reined in and stood among the trees like the ghost Beth had taken him to be. Five minutes, no more. Two riders came into view. One was a tall *hombre* decked out in black like a funeral director, the other was McGill, the Pinkerton agent. McGill was wearing his neat bowler and his fancy waistcoat. The tall *hombre* was tooled up and had a Winchester in a sheath beside his saddle. Both rode with steady purpose just out of sight of Beth's buckboard.

Jordan let them pass and then urged Regius out of the cover of the trees. Before he came up close behind them, the tall man in the dark outfit glanced back over his shoulder and saw him. He and McGill reined in and turned.

'Ah, Mr Jordan!' McGill shouted. 'So we meet again and so soon too.'

Jordan drew in beside him. 'It seems you're going my way, McGill,' he said. 'How come?'

McGill wasn't an easy man to put out. Smiling under his bowler, he looked almost like a benign Humpty Dumpty. The other man frowned: he was obviously none too keen to have the tables turned on him.

'Thought we might check a few things out,' McGill said. 'This gentleman here is Mr Pike, sometimes known as Rig.'

'Glad to meet you, Mr Jordan,' Pike said more as an acknowledgement than as a greeting. 'You headed Redsville way?'

'Escorting a lady,' Jordan said.

'Nice country up there,' McGill said.

'Real nice,' Jordan rejoined.

McGill was smiling broadly but Jordan saw from something in his eyes that he wasn't entirely to be trusted.

'You still got my card?' McGill said.

Jordan nodded. 'Tucked away inside my pocket. I keep it with my gold watch.'

McGill laughed, a rather unpleasant gurgling laugh. 'Don't forget my offer. There could be a big reward for the right man.'

'As I said, I'll keep that in mind,' Jordan said.

'I have an office in Redsville,' McGill said. 'Quite small, but it keeps me up to date with what's happening up there. You could visit with me sometime maybe.'

'I'll bear that in mind,' Jordan said.

Pike grinned but said nothing.

'Well, *adios* then,' McGill said. 'Be seeing you later.' He wheeled his horse round to face the opposite direction.

Pike did the same. He glanced down at the peacemaker at Jordan's side and raised his eyebrows as if he wondered whether Jordan could use it.

The two man rode away like silent effigies.

'Were those men following us?' Beth asked wide-eyed as he caught up with the buckboard.

'Not you,' he assured her. 'It's me they're interested in.'

'You wouldn't be in trouble, would you, Mr Nat Jordan?' She showed a row of pearly white teeth.

The driver said nothing, but Jordan could see by the turning of his head that he was listening.

'What do you aim to do when we get to our place?' Beth asked.

'Probably I'll ride on to the family spread, see how they welcome me after all this time.'

She glanced at him sideways. 'You haven't asked me much about the family. Is that because you don't want to listen, or you'd rather not hear?'

Jordan shrugged. 'You told me about my pa and my brother Rick,' he said. This girl Beth had a deal of savvy. 'I have ears,' he continued, 'it's always good to listen.'

'Well,' she said. 'Your father is apoplectic in his rages, like I said. But my pa gets along with him just fine. Your ma is long suffering and kind. Everyone respects her in the neighbourhood. Two of your sisters got married and left. Cary carries most of the burden of the farm. And Rick is in California like I said. Rick was always the dreamer in the family, but I don't have to tell you that. He finally woke up from his dreams and left.'

It was the longest speech she had uttered so far. Was she poking gentle fun at him? he wondered.

When the Armitage farm came into view. Jordan felt a shiver of apprehension in his spine; like he was a swimmer going down for the third time and having flashes of his past life. He suddenly remembered chasing Beth down by the creek when she was no more than a skinny kid. A strange feeling of excitement came back to him.

Beth smiled shyly as though she remembered it too. 'Why don't you come in for a bite before you ride on? I'm sure Mom and Pa would be pleased to see you after so long.'

'I'd be glad to say hello to them,' he said. He remembered Beth's old man who smiled even when he was riled up. And her mother too, a woman always ready to welcome a stranger.

As they rode up to the house, the husband and wife came

out onto the veranda, squinting and cupping their eyes to see who this stranger was.

'Well I'll be darned tootin!' Beth's father exclaimed, and her mother threw up her hands in astonishment. To Jordan's surprise they both looked older and a little faded like pictures that had fallen unexpectedly out of an album.

Beth's mother ran forward as Jordan swept off his new Stetson. 'Is it you, Nat Jordan,' she exclaimed, 'or a man from the world of shadows?'

'It's me, Mrs Armitage,' he admitted.

'We met in the city,' Beth explained needlessly. 'Just think of it!'

The old man seized his hand and wrung it tight. 'You went away a boy,' he said, 'and you come back a seasoned man.'

'Well, now,' Beth's mother said, 'you must come right inside and sit yourself down and have yourself some chuck.'

'I'm on my way home,' Jordan said. 'Aim to get there before sundown.' He pictured his old man sitting out on the veranda with his white beard flowing with wild assertiveness.

They went into the house, all homey and snug as he remembered. In the kitchen there was a long deal table that served all purposes and a stand-up clock that chimed on the hour. There was a pervading smell of good food and wholesomeness.

They sat at the table and ate the large cookies for which Beth's mother was famous.

'Well, I'll be darn tootin!' Beth's father said again. 'Your old dad'll be so pleased to see you. The return of the prodigal after all these years. When he spies you coming he'll send word to kill the fatted calf.' He leaned forward and screwed up his eyes. 'You bin wounded, or something to keep you away? Your old man never stops talking about you and grieving over you even to this day. Thinks you must have died a hero on the battlefield.'

Jordan nodded. 'I'm no hero, Mr Armitage, but I nearly died once or twice, that's for sure. '

His mind flashed back to the incident in the barn with Coulter and to other narrow escapes he'd had.

'Well you're back now, that's clear enough,' Mrs Armitage exclaimed. 'You must ride over and visit with us right soon.'

Jordan went out and took Regius's reins. He turned and saw Beth framed in the doorway. She wasn't quite out nor quite in; she just stood there looking halfway shy and half bold.

'You take good care, Mr Jordan,' she said quietly.

As he mounted up, another rider emerged from the barn close by. It was the 'breed who had driven the buckboard back from Kansas City.

'Mind if I ride along with you, Mr Jordan?' he said laconically; it was the first time Jordan had heard him utter a word. Jordan noticed the man had a Winchester carbine in a saddle holster close by his saddle.

'You reckon I need a nursemaid?' he asked.

The man inclined his head. 'Just an extra gun if you need it,' he answered solemnly. 'Name's Mex. That's what they call me. Mr Armitage asked me to ride along with you.'

'Just for the company?' Jordan suggested.

'Just for the company,' the man agreed.

Mex was no big talker. They rode on in silence for a while.

'You been around long?' Jordan asked.

'A piece,' said Mex. 'Work for Mr Armitage. He treats me good.'

Now Jordan had the chance to look at him he saw that Mex had a lean, hungry face under the sombrero he chose to wear. Mex stared ahead as though he had seen most things and didn't like many of the things that came into view.

But Jordan had his mind on other things, like how would his father act when he saw them approaching the spread. He thought of Mrs Armitage's kitchen and the warm feeling that prevailed there. He wondered if his mother's kitchen exuded a similar welcoming smell.

The homestead lay in a clearing just below a stand of trees. An ideal spot, he thought. Why would a man leave a place like this to fight a war? he wondered.

Way before the buildings came into view, he had that strange creepy feeling in his spine like he had before the opening shots of a battle. Could be just nerves. Yet, as soon as he saw the place, he stiffened. Feels like there's something terribly wrong here, he thought. He could tell from the way Mex fingered the butt of his carbine that he sensed it too. As they reached the crest of the hill, they saw it: a battered farmhouse with the door hanging wide open, on the porch a rocking-chair hurled on its side.

Mex drew his Winchester and looked round warily. Jordan rode forward to the veranda where his father should have been rising to greet him, but now the rocking chair lay there overturned and abandoned.

Jordan dismounted and went on into the house. Nothing but overturned broken chairs. Even the long table had been capsized and axed.

He went on into the room and saw what he had dreaded but in his heart knew he would find: his father's body swinging on the end of a rope suspended from a beam above.

The old man's body swung to and fro with a sickening creak. His neck was twisted and his head hung down grotesquely. His white beard flamed out from his sagging jaw. His eyes were protruding and, as his body swung round, he seemed to stare at his son, in horrified and accusing amazement.

43

CHAPTER FOUR

Jordan turned and saw Mex standing in the doorway. Mex was trailing the Winchester carbine in his left hand. He removed his sombrero and held it close to his chest. He looked up at the dead man with an expression of puzzlement. He hung the hat on the leg of a broken chair and traced the sign of the cross on his chest.

'This is bad,' he muttered. 'This is the worst.'

Jordan stood in a daze of unreality. He couldn't take in the truth of what had happened: his father's body swinging from the rafters with his head wrenched to one side, the ghastly look of outrage frozen on his face.

Then he saw a kind of scroll nailed to a post. He reached out and tore it away. He unrolled it and read what it said:

Let this be a lesson to all traitors. If you undermine the cause this is what will happen to you. BE WARNED.
Colonel Quantrill the Second!

Jordan handed the scroll to Mex. Mex looked at it blankly for a moment and then handed it back without a word.

Colonel Quantrill the Second!

Jordan was still trying to get his head round what had happened. He had seen many men who had died in battle, some of them close buddies, some crying out for their mothers, some just curling up and vomiting blood, but seeing his father swinging there from the beam in his own home was something altogether more horrific.

Mex brought him back to reality by finding another overturned chair. He placed it close to the swinging body and produced a bowie knife. Jordan put his arms round his father's already stiffened body and steadied it while Mex sliced at the rope. Then together they lowered the body and laid it on the table. It seemed pitifully small and frail like an empty shell. Been dead since morning, Jordan thought. And it wasn't a quick death either. The old man must have swung and kicked out frantically, seeking for some way to save himself. That was a truly terrible end for anyone, let alone a man's own father.

Mex went to the door and looked out holding his Winchester close. 'Soon be sundown,' he said. 'I think I go fetch the buckboard. Can't leave your father here. We must show respect.'

A practical man, Jordan thought. A good man to have at your side in this or any kind of crisis.

As they went out onto the veranda they heard muffled cries.

'In the barn!' Mex said.

The raiders had tried to set fire to the barn but someone or something had stopped them. That was where the muffled cries were coming from. Mex and Jordan wrenched open the door. There were two women inside with their arms tied behind their backs.

'My God, save us!' Jordan's sister Cary begged as they pushed their way in.

The other woman moaned and keened. It was Jordan's mother.

Mex cut through Cary's bonds with his bowie knife and Jordan stooped to comfort his trembling mother.

45

'Who are you?' she cried.

'It's me, Nathaniel,' he soothed.

Cary was on her feet already, rubbing the circulation back into her wrists. 'Oh, Mex,' she said, 'you came at last. Thank God!' She looked at Jordan. 'You're not Nat!' she exclaimed. 'Nat's dead. He died in the war!' She seemed almost delirious with terror and grief.

'I'm Nat,' Jordan assured her. 'I came home.'

'Home,' his mother moaned. 'We have no home for you. What happened to your father? They kept him in the house and beat him!'

Cary was studying him keenly. Now she had heard his voice she recognized him for sure.

'I think we get you back to the Armitage place,' Mex suggested calmly.

'But where's your father?' Jordan's mother insisted. 'I must go to him!'

Jordan put his hands on her frail shoulders and held her close. 'You can't go into the house: it's been ransacked. We need to get you to the Armitages' so they can take care of you.'

'But I can't do that! Your father needs me! I must go to him!' she screamed.

'You can't help Father,' Jordan said. 'Father's past help. He's dead.'

'They killed Father!' wailed Cary. 'Those wild men killed him!' she sobbed.

Back at the Armitages' the two women were hurried in. Nobody could have been kinder; nobody could have had better neighbours.

Jordan and Mex had covered the body and brought it back to the Armitages' homestead on the buckboard. Beth's mother went about the place preparing beds and making sympathetic noises. Old Man Armitage got out his shotgun and loaded it up together with a variety of older weapons he had stored around the place like he was expecting a siege.

Cary wanted to talk, couldn't help talking about what had happened. It was her way of expressing her grief. Jordan listened and took note of all she said. The dam of grief hadn't burst in him yet. He was still numb but his head was as clear as a mountain stream.

According to Cary's account they came in the first light of dawn. She hadn't been able to number them but there were at least fifteen riders. They drew up in front of the place and tied their horses to the veranda rail just like they were about to make a social call. In fact, at first it seemed as friendly as a neighbourly visit.

Jordan's father told the women to stand aside. He was about to go out and greet the visitors. The night before he had delivered a political speech in Redsville; all about how the Union cause had been vindicated and the Confederates had been defeated and now they should concentrate on building up the community for the good of the Union. No more injustice, no more slavery. The old man was firmly opposed to any kind of slavery, though he was a tyrant in his own home. He had decided to stand for the House in the next election. Despite his age and his old-time flowing beard he had his following too; maybe he would make governor.

When the raiders pushed their way into the place he was halfway to meeting them. He had a welcoming smile on his face when Quantrill the Second, alias Coulter, stepped over the threshold. There was something about the man his followers called *Colt* that froze the marrow in a person's bones. Not that he was villainous or rude; if anything, he was over polite.

He stood there with a wide smile under the black stetson he hadn't bothered to remove in the house and greeted the old man. 'Well now, Mr Jordan, it seems the day of reckoning has come.'

'Is that so?' the old man answered bluntly. 'And whose day of reckoning would that be, mister?'

'Why yours, of course, Mr Jordan. *The Judgement of the Lord is nigh* as it says in the Good Book.'

'The judgement of the Lord is always just around the corner,' old man Jordan chimed.

The other man grinned. 'But it's a little closer to you than you think, Mr Jordan. Fact is at this moment it's staring you right in the face.'

The old man turned the colour of a well-seasoned cheese. 'When the Lord comes, I hope I'm ready to receive Him,' he said, thrusting his beard out at Coulter.

Coulter raised his head and laughed. 'Unfortunately the Lord is a little busy right now, so He sent me instead to deputize.'

Coulter turned to the men crowding in at the door with a laugh. Most of them were carrying Winchesters and one had a coil of rope dangling from his hands. 'Get these women out of here!' Coulter ordered.

Mrs Jordan screamed and Cary protested. 'What do you mean, barging into a God-fearing house and frightening everybody to death like this?' she said.

'*To death*,' Coulter said. 'That is the point, ma'am: to death it is.'

Three of the raiders strode forward and roughly grabbed the two women, both of whom immediately started to scratch and fight. Cary lashed out like a middle weight champion and knocked one of her assailants to the ground. But she was quickly overpowered. Then both women were tied up with their hands behind their backs.

The old man had tried to intervene but one of the raiders stepped in quickly and butted him down with the stock of his Winchester. Jordan senior fell to the ground, clutching his middle, winded.

The women were carried off screaming to the barn and locked inside.

After that, it was all speculation but the conclusion was obvious. The old man was trussed up. They put a noose around his neck and threw the other end of the rope over a beam. Coulter delivered sentence:

'We don't want to do this, Mr Jordan, but we have concluded you are a danger to the community. We represent the southern cause which is not defeated despite the recent war. You are an enemy of the people and so you must hang by the neck until you die.'

So the raiders hauled old Jordan up onto the beam and let him hang, kicking and jerking out his life. With such a short drop a man can take an awful long time to die. His neck is not broken and he struggles to keep alive until the darkness overtakes him and he hangs motionless and lifeless like a dead bird in a tree.

The raiders then talked about setting fire to the house and the barn but changed their minds before the flames took hold.

'Now, boys!' Coulter said. 'We're about justice here. We don't want to be vindictive, do we? After all, we're men of principle, not barbarians.'

Then he hammered in the scroll that told why the so-called execution had taken place.

Next morning the Armitages and the Jordans sat grieving around the long table in the Armitages' place. Everyone knew that something had to be done, but nobody knew what or how to do it. Beth's mother was busy trying to keep them fed. Her father wanted to say *well, I'll be dang tootin* repeatedly but kept himself quiet out of respect for the dead. Beth was comforting Nat Jordan's mother and his sister Cary. Cary couldn't keep herself still. She kept staring out of the window and moving around the table like a woman possessed.

It was Nat Jordan who saw the riders approaching over the ridge. Had Coulter and his raiders come back for another kill? He reached out and strapped on his gunbelt. Old man Armitage seized his shotgun and stuck an old Navy Colt through his waistband. Everyone got up from the table and started to panic.

'No need to trouble yourselves,' Mex said from the door. He was carrying his Winchester. 'It's Sheriff Stevenoak. Seems he's come with a posse.'

The riders rode right up to the door and dismounted. Stevenoak, a big man with a tightly groomed beard, stepped inside. 'Have no fear,' he boomed. 'We come in to investigate a crime and ride down the killers. Is it OK to bring my men inside, Mr Armitage?'

Sure it was OK. There was a collective sigh of relief. The law was here to give protection and cover. Everyone could breathe easy at last.

The sheriff came in looking morbidly grieved just like he had lost his own father. 'Heard rumours of the attack,' he said. 'Came up just as soon as we could. Mrs Jordan . . . This is such a grievous thing to have happened.' He went over to Jordan's mother and squeezed her tight. Jordan heard the breath escape from her like she had been crushed by a grizzly.

The other members of the posse came into the living-room and stood around like they didn't know what to do or say. Outside on the porch, almost as if he was keeping himself hidden, Jordan saw McGill, the Pinkerton agent, and his side kick, the man dressed in black called Pike, or Rig.

'This is a terrible thing happening in the territory,' Stevenoak said.

'How did you hear about what happened and so

quickly?' Beth's father asked him.

Stevenoak rubbed his stubbly jaw. 'Neighbour was watching from the cover of the woods. Saw everything. Watched those renegades ride by. Rode into Redsville just as soon as he could. That's why we're here. Got to stamp out this fire before it spreads and rages through the whole county. What with the train hold-up and this, no man or woman or child can sleep safe in their beds.' At the end of this speech the sheriff was clean out of breath. Mrs Armitage handed him a glass of home-brew and he downed it in one long draught. 'This is strictly out of my territory,' he said. 'But here we have to make an exception. Man stands idle, things get worse. We have to stamp this evil out once and for all!'

There was a murmur approval from everyone round the table, members of the posse included.

'You hear what the man says?' McGill spoke quietly. He had sidled up to Jordan and touched his arm.

Jordan turned and looked at him. The same expansive belly, the same gold watch chain, the same fancy waistcoat though now he had had the grace remove his dark bowler. And he wasn't smoking a cigar.

'I hear what the man says,' Jordan replied with scant politeness.

McGill nodded as though he understood the need for respect in the face of tragedy. 'I'm deeply sorry to hear about your pa,' he said unctuously. 'I hear he was a good man, and nobody deserves to die like that.'

Jordan made no reply. Something about the Pinkerton agent offended him, but he couldn't figure what.

'Tell you the truth,' McGill continued, 'I couldn't quite make you out when we met. But now I have you figured.'

Jordan narrowed his eyes. He could see the swarthy, black-clad form of Pike hovering just beyond. 'What have you in mind?' he asked McGill.

51

McGill looked up thoughtfully. 'Well, it's like this, Mr Jordan. My guess is you know this man Coulter rather well from the past. Would I be right in thinking he was one of your old comrades in the recent war?'

His ferret eyes wandered over Jordan quickly. Jordan stared back at him hard.

'Could be he was your commanding officer one time,' McGill pressed. 'Would that be true as well?'

Jordan averted his gaze and saw Beth watching him with her grey-blue, rather attractive eyes.

'Old comrades,' McGill muttered. 'War is funny that way. It makes enemies of men, but it also brings comrades together in brotherhood. Ain't that so?'

Jordan gave a brief nod, but still he said nothing. He felt Beth's gaze trying to reach out and comfort him as Sheriff Stevenoak continued booming on with specious words of solace.

'A link that once forged cannot be broken easily,' McGill was muttering. 'Would that be right, Mr Jordan?'

Jordan turned to him quickly. 'Don't bullshit me, Mr McGill. I'm not in the mood.'

McGill paused to take a breath. Then he raised his hand. 'Oh, I know, I know,' he said. 'Believe me, I understand. I lost my own pa recently. It's a hard thing to take.'

Jordan felt rather than saw Beth almost at his side.

McGill drew back slightly. 'You still got my card, Mr Jordan,' he said. 'As I think I mentioned we have an office in Redsville. Think things over. When you recover a little from your father's cruel murder, drop in so we can talk.'

He turned away, nodded to Pike, the man in black, and made his way down to the veranda rail to untie his horse.

Beth stood so close to Jordan he almost felt her sweet breath on his cheek. 'Who is that man?' she asked.

Jordan turned to look at her and saw something he

hadn't noticed before: there were small flecks of gold in the grey-blue of her eyes.

'Pinkerton agent,' he said but he was no longer thinking about McGill.

Beth shook her head slightly, but kept her eyes on him. 'I don't like that man,' she said. 'There's something sinister about him. And the man who wears black: he's like a dark shadow.'

Now he looked from her eyes to her lips which were full and ripe. 'McGill's sinister,' he admitted. 'Like an old crow perched on a rotting stump. It goes with the territory.' He didn't mention Pike who made his blood creep even more.

Beth smiled. 'An old crow on a rotting stump, that's a good phrase,' she said. She took a breath. 'I'm so sorry about your pa.'

The words struck at his heart like the bite of a snake. Coming from Beth they seemed uniquely sincere.

He turned away and walked to the corner of the house.

There was the murmur of faint breeze on the prairie.

A dark figure stood by the barn door. It shaped itself as Mex.

'What do you aim to do?' Mex said quietly.

Mex's low but determined voice concentrated the mind. Jordan asked himself the same question: what did he aim to do? He needed to think about his folks, his distressed ma and his sister Cary, the body of his pa swinging from the beam with that accusing look in his eye.

'I guess I have to ride in on those killers,' he said. 'One way or another I have to find out where they are.'

Though he couldn't see Mex dearly, he felt his hard-lined face relax into a half smile 'I'd like to ride with you on that one,' Mex said.

CHAPTER FIVE

Someone had to ride into Redsville, make arrangements for the old man to receive a proper burial.

Guess that's my job, Jordan thought.

'Maybe you should stay around here,' Mrs Armitage said. 'In case those vengeful varmints come back again.'

'They won't come back in a hurry,' old man Armitage said. 'They done their worst. Now they'll be looking for the next target. Ain't that so, Nat?'

Jordan conceded that it was so and strapped on his gunbelt.

Mex said he intended to go with Jordan and, though there was plenty to do around the place, Armitage agreed. 'Maybe you two hot-heads can keep one another out of trouble,' he said.

So Mex strapped on a gunbelt too and he and Jordan mounted up ready to go.

Cary and Beth were on the porch. Cary was carrying one of Armitage's ancient pistols.

'You take care now,' she called. She seemed to have got hold of herself since the shock of her father's death and the gun in her hand gave her another way of channelling her grief. Jordan guessed she would have liked to be riding with him, but thought it best to stay and look after her grieving mother.

Beth stood on the step looking up at Jordan. Watch after yourself, her expression said. Jordan felt something inside him move like the plates of the earth. He nodded briefly and he and Mex rode on.

'See you got yourself tooled up,' Jordan said to Mex.

Mex nodded. 'Man's got to be ready,' he said between his teeth.

'You had occasion to use that hardware much?' Jordan asked him.

Mex turned and squinted at him. 'I can use a gun,' he said. 'Had to learn when I was young. *Bandidos* killed my pa when I was a kid. Had to defend the cabin. Got two of them but they shot my pa.' He rode on in silence for while. 'Your old man offended folks a deal, but not enough to be killed like that. Mr Jordan was a good man.'

Again they rode in silence for while.

'You ever shot a Negro?' Mex asked suddenly.

Jordan turned to look at him but Mex gave no sign.

'Might have done,' Jordan admitted. 'Not because his skin was black but because he was on the other side in the war. A man kills or dies in a battle and it doesn't figure what colour his skin is. That's the way it swings.'

Mex nodded. 'Why I asked is I understand you fought with the Rebs. Your father was a Unionist man. How come?'

Jordan gave a faint intake of breath, not quite a sigh. 'At the time it seemed the right thing to do. My pa and me couldn't agree about many things. So I went to fight for the Rebs. I didn't like the way those Yankees were dominating everything.'

'Do you regret that now?' Mex asked from the corner of his mouth.

Jordan rode on considering the matter. 'I think you just asked the wrong question,' he said.

'That could be so,' Mex admitted.

'Speak what's on your mind,' Jordan said.

Mex wasn't a talking man. He struggled with his words for a while. Then he said, 'OK, *señor*. So you fought with the Rebs and against the Union. Your pa was a Union man and you were a Reb. What will you do when you catch up on those Rebs who killed your pa?'

A very good question. Jordan thought about it, but for a while he said nothing. His mind went right back to the war again.

Jordan and Coulter were sleeping in a barn. They had crept in and pulled straw over themselves to keep out the cold in the middle of a bitter night. The weather was sharp and they hadn't eaten for two days. They had been running and crawling to avoid the Yankees. They were somewhere behind the lines and if you gave yourself up to a bunch of wild troopers you could be shot down on the spot or strung up to the nearest tree. It was a bloody, gruesome war.

'You hear something?' Coulter whispered.

Jordan was already up on one elbow with his gun cocked. He had heard distant voices coming closer. It was now full daylight.

Coulter was on his feet with his gun held ready. He went over to the door and squinted out, right into the eyes of a woman who was about to come into the barn. She opened her mouth to scream and he batted her down with the butt of his gun. She fell back screaming. Coulter went to shoot her but it was already too late. The approaching soldiers were right close.

Jordan was at the door. He saw the woman, middle-aged, a farmer's wife writhing on the ground with her hand clawing at her mouth which was spouting blood. She must have lost a tooth or two but she was still screaming.

'We must git!' Coulter said.

But it was too late. Half-a-dozen men in blue uniforms came riding and circling close with guns trained on Coulter.

'Drop those guns!' an officer shouted. 'Drop those guns and get your hands in the air!'

Jordan was ready to shoot it out, but it was a matter of surrender or die.

Coulter hesitated. This was decision time. 'OK,' he shouted. 'I'm Captain Coulter. You kill me or my partner you offend against the conventions of war!'

The officer who had shouted the order brought out a great guffaw of laughter. 'Conventions of law, my arse!' he shouted. 'You're Captain Coulter. I'm General Confusion. We don't have no conventions of war in this neck of the woods.'

Jordan saw that the advancing soldiers were about to open fire. The woman crawling on the ground screamed out, 'Don't shoot! Spare us! I got young uns in the house.'

The officer on the horse let out another bellow of laughter. 'You got young uns; I got young uns; all God's children got young uns,' he sang out.

The soldiers started to jeer and sing.

'You young uns gonna drop your weapons, or do we have to shoot you where you stand?' the officer demanded.

Coulter glanced sideways at Jordan. 'They gonna kill us, they gonna kills us,' he muttered. He dropped his weapon to the straw. Jordan laid his gun on the ground and raised his hands.

'Wise choice,' said the officer, riding close. 'OK, boys, get these turkeys trussed up ready for the oven. We got work to do.'

Soldiers sprang up from everywhere and started to advance with their sights on the two Rebs. The woman scrambled up moaning and dabbing at her bloody face.

Good job Coulter slugged her, Jordan thought. That might have saved her life.

The officer – he was a captain, Jordan saw – gestured with his gun. 'Take the woman inside. Rustle up some grub in there.'

The Yankee soldiers, most of them nothing but smooth-chinned boys, were pawing Jordan and Coulter all over like they might have porcupine quills. Then a sergeant took charge and had the two captives tied up good and tight with their hands behind their backs.

'What do we do with them, Captain?' the sergeant said. 'You want we string them up, or take them along with us?'

The captain looked over Coulter with a sneer. 'Some captain, I'd say.' He struck Coulter across the face with his glove.

He moved to Jordan. 'Where you from, Soldier?'

'West,' Jordan said. 'Other side of the Mississippi.'

'Well, one thing's for certain,' the captain said, 'you ain't gonna see those rolling plains of home again, and that's for sure.' He turned to the sergeant and barked out an order. 'Put a guard on these weasels while we go into the farm and relax and eat.'

The sergeant wasn't taking any chances. He assigned two rankers to watch the bound men and then followed the captain into the house.

'They're just as sick of the war as we are,' Jordan said.

'They might be sick but that don't stop a man being mad,' Coulter said. 'Question is, is that captain and that sergeant mad enough to kill us?'

Depends on how much booze the old woman's got in her still, Jordan thought. They drink too much and sleep it off, we might have a chance. They drink just enough to rile themselves up, they'll probably hang us. Either way things

58

don't look good.

Coulter was obviously thinking along the same lines. He was looking at the two rookies who had been assigned to watch over them. One of them was unwholesome-looking and fat like a porker. The other had a young farm-boy face. Both looked relatively stupid but that doesn't stop a boy or a man from being a mean soldier.

When the two were talking about how they could murder some of that booze the captain and sergeant and the other rankers were drinking, Coulter was working his wrist up and down against a knife he had hidden in his boot. Though they had tied him up good and tight, he had kept his fists clenched so there was still a little play in his hands: an old trick.

The porky young soldier came to the door of the barn and looked down at his two captives with a sneer across his lips. 'You ready for your glory day?' he said in a high, syrupy tone.

'Just about as ready as you,' Coulter replied.

'Don't look much like a soldier to me,' piggy boy said. 'Look more like a rat just crawled out from behind a barn ready to be shot.'

The other sentry seemed to think that was funny and they both hooted away for almost a whole minute.

'You pissed yourself yet?' the other sentry asked. 'They say a man pisses hisself when he's going to die. I seen it myself.'

'You must have pissed yourself a dozen times,' Coulter laughed. 'I can smell it even from here.'

That didn't please the farm boy. He looked at the fat boy and didn't know what to say. The fat boy rattled his musket and pointed it at Coulter. 'You talk a lot of crap for a rat in a trap!' he said menacingly. He bent right over Coulter to intimidate him more . . . a little too close.

59

Coulter struck out with his boot and sent the piggy boy right back against the door post. He hit the post so hard the whole barn shook itself like a dog and the pig-faced soldier slid down like a sack of potatoes and landed pie-eyed on a pile of straw. He shook his head like he was trying to shake off a bad hangover and careered over sideways.

The other soldier stood in the doorway waving his musket and bellowing. Jordan was on his feet. He ran forward and lunged at the boy, butting him low on the chest with his head. The farm boy gave a grunt of dismay as he fell but Coulter was already onto him, kicking down on his face and chest.

To Jordan's surprise, Coulter had managed to work his hands free. He stooped and grabbed the soldier's gun. He cocked it and was about to discharge it in the kid's face, when Jordan held him back. 'You shoot the boy, those soldiers will come bursting out like a swarm of hornets! Better we grab the horses and ride!'

Coulter didn't wait for further explanations. They ran over to where the horses were tethered by the ranch house and grabbed them away. Coulter did most of the grabbing since Jordan's hands were still tied. Coulter worked quickly to pick out the best horses and stampede the rest away.

The door of the ranch house sprang open and the sergeant ran out with his mouth full of pie and a gun in his hand. It was the last pie he ever ate. Coulter swung the musket on him and pulled the trigger. There was a mighty explosion and the sergeant bucked back and fell against the captain who also had his mouth full.

Coulter was already on a horse, but mounting a horse with your hands tied behind your back is no easy feat. So Jordan was half on and half off a horse's back. Coulter could have got away clean, but he leaned over, grabbed Jordan by the belt and hoisted him onto the horse's back. Jordan bit the reins with his teeth, and they rode.

They had the luck of the devil on that ride. Coulter had managed to stampede most of the army horses. The sergeant had fallen across the doorway. He was a big man. So it took a few valuable moments before the captain and the troopers could get clear and break out of the cabin.

'That was Satan's luck!' Coulter shouted, as he and Jordan galloped away. 'See how much pie those gut masters' had stuffed into their faces?'

Jordan didn't reply. He was too busy gripping the reins between his teeth!

Jordan and Mex rode into the small town of Redsville. Jordan remembered it well from when he was a boy and it hadn't changed much: just the basic services, the sheriff's office, a small schoolhouse, a store that sold most everything you could need except what you had to go to Kansas City for, and a building that called itself a funeral parlour.

'Why don't you go to the store?' Jordan said to Mex. 'They run a small coffee shop in there. You could take a drink.'

Mex pulled a wry face. 'All the same to you, I'll stick around. Some folks ain't too friendly with Mexicans in this town.'

Jordan nodded and rode on to the funeral parlour. Inside he saw a man with his sleeves rolled back shaping a coffin. The man looked up and a flicker of recognition crossed his glowing face. 'Ah, Nat Jordan unless I'm mistaken! If I didn't know you come back, I might have thought you were a ghost.'

'No ghost, Jonathan. I'm here on business.'

The funeral director's face took on a serious expression. 'Sorry to hear about your pa. He was a good man though he did do a deal of ranting.'

'Yes, he was,' Jordan agreed. 'Maybe you could spare the time to come up to the place and bury him.'

Jonathan Fawcett laid aside his measuring rule and nodded gravely. 'I'll do that, Nat. It'll be an a honour. A man like your father deserves the best burial we can give him.'

There wasn't much choice over the wood for the coffin. So Jordan went over to the Washington Hotel. It was the only hotel in town and it had a saloon that was open most of the day. As soon as he pushed open the door he heard the familiar sound of fiddle playing. Preacher Man was sitting on a stool by the well-polished bar. He was just finishing *Barbara Allen,* one of his most melancholy tunes. He wore his curly bowler at a jaunty angle and he was sporting the same check suit he had been wearing when Jordan met him on the railroad train.

'Why, who comes here!' Preacher Man shouted as the notes of the song died away. 'Howdy, pardner! Howdy!'

Jordan went over to the bar and ordered himself a beer and another for Mex.

'Heard about the man they strung up,' Preacher Man said. 'Someone just told me it was your pa. I'm real sorry to hear that.'

Jordan gave him a straight look. 'What brings you here?' he asked the fiddler. 'Redsville isn't the place to make a man rich.'

'You got me wrong, pardner,' Preacher Man sang out. 'A man don't aim to get rich; a man aims to please himself and other folks too. I just fix it to give a concert here. All the old songs. You should come along. Like your old man would be glad for you. Shows you're still in the land of hope.' He leaned forward across the bar. 'I come up to the place, or play at the old man's wake, or even at the funeral if that's what you desire.'

'I'll think about it,' Jordan said.

Preacher Man paused. He leaned forward further and held his hand across his mouth. 'Guess you'll be wanting to catch up on those whey-bellies who killed your old man. As you see, I don't carry shooting irons, but who knows, I might be in a position to help you there.'

Jordan glanced across at Mex and gave him a faint nod. 'I think I'll just step across to the other side of the street. I got a word to say to a man.'

He threw back the last of his beer and stood up. Mex made to rise as well, but Jordan steadied him with a wave of his hand.

'*Adios*, partner,' Preacher Man said. 'Be seeing you.'

Jordan adjusted his gunbelt and stood at the door of the Washington. He looked up and down the street and stepped across to the other side where he had seen a sign with the words *Pinkerton Agency*.

He climbed the creaking stairs but there was no need to tap on the door. He had caught the scent of cigar smoke on his way up and he wasn't surprised to see the agent framed in the doorway with a Havana stuck between his teeth.

'Saw you coming across the street,' McGill said. 'Figured you thought things over and wanted to talk. Come into the office and we can lay out our cards.'

The room was more like a cupboard than an office. There was one high window that looked out over the street. Jordan figured McGill had stood there watching and chuckling as he emerged from the Washington, looking both ways before crossing. Like a spider watching a fly, he thought.

He sat down and McGill made himself comfortable in the chair behind his desk and nodded. He was obviously enjoying his cigar. He took his watch out of his waistcoat pocket and gave it a long affectionate look. He smiled in anticipation. 'That Sheriff Stevenoak is just a big bag of shit, you know that?'

Jordan grinned. 'I think I worked that one out for myself.'

'Means well, of course,' McGill continued. 'We all mean well. I think I read somewhere the road to Hell is paved with good intentions. Something like that.'

Jordan waited: he was in no particular hurry.

'Tell you one thing,' the Pinkerton agent continued, 'whatever happens in this county, Stevenoak won't lift a finger. He hasn't got the balls for it.'

'You could be right there,' Jordan agreed.

'He'll roust around the country with a band of armed layabouts pretending to look for those Quantrill Raiders, but he won't find them in a million years. That's because he won't want to find them in case they shoot him from here to kingdom come.'

'That could be true,' Jordan said.

McGill gave him a long appraising look, sending out a stream of rich-smelling smoke from his Havana. Then he took the cigar from between his lips and tapped it on the edge of the table, shaking ash onto the floor. 'I think we might both want the same thing here, Mr Jordan,' he suggested.

'What would that be, Mr McGill?'

McGill smiled as though he liked to play games. Like Jordan he was in no hurry to come to the point.

'I figure it this way,' he said slowly. 'These raiders hung your pa from the rafters of his own cabin. That's an ugly way to go. A man choking out his life has a long time to think.'

Jordan nodded and felt something like a knife twisting in his gut.

'That's part of the story,' McGill continued. 'And the other part is this: a man is riding home on the iron horse.

The horse gets held up. The man on the iron horse recognizes the leader of the raiders and addresses him by name.'

Jordan nodded and waited.

McGill twisted his mouth in a grin. 'What I have to figure is this,' he said. 'How well does the man riding on the iron horse know the hold-up man? Have they been buddies in the recent war? Maybe they are old comrades in arms. How sympathetic to the lost Confederate cause is the man riding on the iron horse? Could he be thinking about throwing in with those raiders? And, if he is, how does he feel when the raiders hang his old man?' McGill leaned forward and scrutinized Jordan intently. 'Those are the questions I have to figure out, Mr Jordan. Maybe you could help me to answer some of them?'

Jordan stirred and got ready to stand. 'I hear what you're saying to me,' he said. 'And I think I catch the drift of your meaning.'

McGill nodded slowly and held his cigar out reflectively. That's good,' he said. 'Only one thing, Mr Jordan, you still don't answer my questions, do you?'

Jordan was on his feet. He looked down at the man sitting behind the desk and wondered why he couldn't like him. 'This matter is personal, Mr McGill,' he said. 'Sure, I knew Coulter once. We fought together and almost died together. As I said, this is a personal matter.'

He went down the stairway and onto the street. He took out his gold watch and consulted its. Almost noon, it told him. He glanced down the street and saw Pike, the man in dark clothes, standing in a doorway smoking a quirly. The man raised a mocking hand and touched the rim of his Stetson. It was Pike who had followed him from Kansas City with McGill – another man he wished he could like.

He crossed the street and went into the Washington. The

first thing he noticed was that Mex had taken in a skinful. Instead of being his usual glum self he was doing a kind of Spanish American dance, clapping his hands above his head and gyrating like a dust devil as Preacher Man scraped away on the fiddle.

Preacher Man looked at Jordan and stopped playing. Mex collided with a table and sat down abruptly in a chair.

'Hi, partner!' Preacher Man said. 'We bin having a ball here since you left.'

'So I see.' Jordan sat down and ordered two plates of food, one for Mex and one for himself. Mex looked slightly discomposed as if he knew he had made himself look like an idiot.

A girl around seventeen came in and plonked the two plates of steak down on the table. Mex looked at his for a moment and started to eat. He was no dandy in his table manners.

The girl brought in another plate for Preacher Man. He was engaged to play the fiddle at the concert and, like in Kansas City, meals were part of the deal.

Jordan had started to carve his steak when he looked up and saw Pike, the man in black, standing just inside the doorway. Pike looked at him and touched the brim of his Stetson again. Jordan saw he had long drooping moustaches and a small beard like a black plaster on his chin. He was wearing a gun in a holster in a way that suggested he knew how to use it and had had plenty of practice.

'You want to talk to me?' Jordan said.

The man tilted his head and gave a kind of sneer. 'It'll wait. Wouldn't want to take your mind of that t-bone steak. Name's Pike, Steve Pike,' he added. 'People call me Rig. Started as kind of a joke and it stuck.'

He sat down at another table and ordered a whiskey.

Mex had slowed down on his eating. Pike or Rig seemed

to have had a calming effect. Preacher Man had calmed down too. He had laid his fiddle aside and was chewing his steak in silence. His table manners, Jordan noticed, were quite dainty compared to Mex's, even a little fancy. Jordan saw that he kept glancing at the black-clad man sideways as though he might make a sudden unexpected move.

Jordan finished his steak.

'You stay here,' he said to Mex, 'but maybe no more dancing, eh?'

He got up and went over to join Pike who was drinking whiskey. 'You had something to say to me?' he said.

Pike chuckled and there was something harsh and throaty in the sound that made the hairs on a man's neck stand on end. 'Always good to talk to a fellow traveller along the road of life,' he said.

He slid the whiskey bottle over to Jordan. 'Have a drink,' he said. 'I got another glass for you. It ain't good whiskey but it'll have to do. Help with your digestion.'

Jordan poured himself a measure.

'I see you don't like to drink,' Pike said.

'It sometimes helps,' Jordan said. 'You work for McGill?' he asked.

The man inclined his head. 'On and off. Mostly I work for myself.' He went on drinking or a moment. 'Could work for you if you had a mind to it,' he added in a low tone.

Jordan rolled the indifferent whiskey around on his tongue. 'What's on your mind? I'm not sure I catch your drift.'

Pike chuckled again in that none-too-pleasant sounding manner. 'You get it, or you don't get it. That's for you. McGill is a good detective. He works on the clues.' He touched the side of his nose. 'I follow this. Like an insect. I home in. And, when I get there, I got this.' He tapped the holster on his thigh and chuckled again. 'This little object knows how to sting.'

Jordan's eyes switched to the holster and the man's hogleg. That is no Sunday decoration, he thought. 'Thanks for the drink,' he said.

He got up from the table. 'I'll keep what you say in mind.'

Pike took a long swig from the bottle. He stood up and raised the bottle in salute. 'You do that, mister,' he said. Something about the way he said it gave Jordan a creepy feeling, like the man had said, take my offer or you could be a dead man.

Jordan returned to the other table where Preacher Man was regaling Mex with tales of horse-thieves and what a man could learn from fiddle playing.

When Jordan glanced towards the door, Pike had disappeared just like he might have been a spectre of the imagination.

'You know something?' Preacher Man murmured apprehensively. 'That hombre is bad medicine.'

He expressed Jordan's feelings perfectly.

'Tell you another thing,' Preacher Man said. 'Remember that guy in Kansas City? The guy at the table on the other side of the room where we had breakfast?'

Jordan remembered the man with his head down pretending to be asleep, the man who had disappeared like smoke without a sound after listening in on their conversation. 'Head down on the table doesn't sound too much like his style,' he said.

'That monkey's got more tricks than a barrelful of snakes,' Preacher Man said.

'That's true,' Mex threw in. The steak had taken off some of the effects of the drink and he was sitting up as alert as a watchful coyote. 'Heard about him and I seen him before. Remembered when he came up to the Armitage place with McGill.'

Jordan looked at Preacher Man and Preacher Man nodded as though he knew about it already.

'You seen him before?' Jordan asked.

'Calls himself Rig,' Mex said. 'Sort of jokey. But that man's no joke. He's a deadly killer. Thinks no more about shooting a man down than squashing a fly on a window pane.'

CHAPTER SIX

Jordan and Mex rode back to the Armitage place in a somewhat reflective mood. Jordan was thinking about the gunman Pike and wondering which way he would jump. Could be he wasn't working for McGill at all. Could be he thought Jordan would lead him to Coulter and the Quantrill bunch. Could even be he was one of the bunch himself and wanted to find out how much Jordan knew.

When they got back to the Armitage place, Old Man Armitage was out in the yard supervising his men. He and several of the hands had been over to the Jordan place to round up the cattle that had been driven off and to put the house to rights as far as they could. Cary had ridden over with them and said she intended to stay in the house. Jordan's mother, still as shaky as a cut leaf birch in the wind, had chosen to stay with the Armitages for a while longer. She couldn't bear the thought of returning to the house where her husband had died so cruelly. Said she would never go back and live there again.

When she heard riders approaching, Beth had come out under the overhang with a shotgun tucked under her arm. And she would have used it, Jordan thought.

When she saw who they were, she sighed with relief and her whole body relaxed and looked happy.

Jordan dismounted and Mex took the horses into the corral.

'You were a long time,' Bess said, looking up into Jordan's eyes. 'I feared something bad might have happened to you.' Jordan saw the flecks of gold darting like fire in her eyes again.

This girl doesn't complain, Jordan thought. Again he experienced that strange unaccustomed feeling somewhere round his heart.

His mother came out of the place and she cried. 'Cary went back to the house,' she said. 'I pray she's safe. I don't think I can ever go back after what they did to your father.'

Jordan put his arms round her and squeezed her frail bones.

They went inside and ate. The Armitage spread was modest, so the hands ate with the family. They were all sitting at the long pine table in the kitchen. Old Man Armitage sat in his usual place at the head of the table and he insisted that Jordan sit opposite him at the other end. Beth sat on Jordan's right beside him.

'What will you do?' she asked quietly, as they proceeded with the meal.

That focused his mind. 'I don't know,' he said. 'I haven't figured it out yet.'

Beth shook her head and pursed her lips. 'I don't believe you,' she said quietly. 'I think you aim to go after those killers and get yourself killed.'

Jordan went on eating for a bit. 'A man doesn't aim to get himself killed,' he said. 'A man aims to do what he thinks is right.'

Beth was smiling to herself. 'I remember what you were like when you were young, how you argued with your pa. That's why you and Rick had to take off.'

Jordan wondered where his brother Rick was now.

Someone had said he had gone to California to look for gold.

'You didn't take much account of me then,' Beth said quietly. 'You just thought I was a long-legged kid with pigtails. And you were right too.' She gave a murmur of laughter. 'I remember how you climbed trees and swam across the river for a bet. That was a real dumb thing to do. You remember that?'

Jordan remembered plunging into the ice-cold river and being carried away in the raging waters. He could picture Beth standing on the bank with her hands to her mouth in a silent scream. He had underrated the current and could have drowned if it hadn't been for a convenient low-hanging branch.

'I remember,' he admitted. He also recalled that the man who had made the bet with him tried to duck out on the deal; how they had fought to a standstill before Jordan got a choke lock on him and forced him to pay up.

'So,' she said, 'whatever you do, you have to keep yourself safe. For your mother, for Cary' – she paused, looking down at her plate – 'and for me too.'

Jordan sat staring down the table at Old Man Armitage for a moment. Something like a chunk of invisible meat had stuck in his throat and he couldn't turn to look at Beth though he saw that she was looking down at the table as if she had amazed herself with what she had said.

He saw her hand close to his but he made no move.

The Jordan funeral went off really well. Nat Jordan was surprised by how popular his father had become with those who favoured the Union cause. There was a good deal of singing and a lot of alleluias. An old friend and associate of Jordan made a grand speech of praise. Preacher Man came too and he played melancholy music Nat Jordan hadn't heard before: Handel or some such. Though the ceremony was both joyful and sad, there was a feeling of uneasiness in the air. Is this the beginning of another phase in the recent war? people asked. Will those raiders come back again and ravage around Redsville? Although many regarded the old man as a hero, even as a kind of martyr, some thought he was a liability to the community. Let sleeping dogs lie and let the Union heal itself, they said.

Though Nat was one of the chief mourners many looked on him with suspicion. Who was this tough, hard-featured ex-soldier who had loomed up like a ghost from the past on the very same day his father was lynched?

One old-timer Jordan remembered dimly from the past sidled up to him with a look of downright suspicion.

'So your old man died with a rope around his neck,' he said in a murmur, so none of the other mourners would hear.

Jordan glanced at him sideways. 'Life is full of coincidences,' he said.

'That is so,' the man reflected in some surprise. 'Like you both being on different sides in the war. That what you mean?' He was grinning and showing a set of yellow dog-like teeth under his whiskers.

Jordan turned to him slowly. 'That was no coincidence. That was a matter of principle,' he said.

The yellow teeth gleamed. 'Just like your pa,' he said. 'I see the firebrand in you, Nat Jordan.'

Jordan figured the yellow teeth needed an argument in spite of the sad occasion. But at that moment Beth came to his rescue again. 'I think we have to go through to the Washington,' she said. 'They laid on a few things to eat. I hope you'll join us there, Mr Proctor.'

She took Nat's arm and they strolled together out of the small log church and across to the hotel. Jordan had a

73

strange, unfamiliar feeling. This girl in pigtails had become a remarkably self-possessed woman. Having a female on his arm was an unfamiliar experience. Was it a pleasure or an embarrassment? Or maybe both? he wondered awkwardly.

'Don't pay heed to that old reptile Proctor,' Beth whispered. 'He'd pick a quarrel with an alligator as long as he wasn't close enough to feel its bite.'

Jordan grinned and nodded. Beth squeezed his arm and moved away as Preacher Man appeared, still holding his beloved fiddle.

'Thanks for playing at the old man's funeral,' Jordan said. 'You chose the right music too.'

'Don't usually go to funerals,' Preacher Man said. 'Don't care for all the emotion involved. But in this case, it seemed a kind of duty since we met on that ill-fated train.'

The Washington had laid on quite a spread in honour of the deceased hero. Before they sat down at table, Preacher Man had something more to say. He leaned in on Jordan and thrust something into his hand. 'I need to give you this,' he said.

Jordan looked down at the crumpled envelope in his hand. 'What is it?' he said.

Preacher Man drew in closer. 'I don't know, but I can guess. While I was fiddling in the hotel the other night a skinny kid came right up to me and gave it to me. The boy said, "You a buddy of Mr Nat Jordan, sir?" I said, "I think I might claim that honor." The kid said, "A man asked me to give you this for him." Then he gave me this letter and, before I could ask him about the man who had given it to him, he just turned away, and drifted off real quick like he didn't want to attract too much attention to himself.'

Jordan looked down at the envelope and saw it was addressed to him in a formal hand he thought he should recognize. He nodded to Preacher Man and stuffed the envelope into his pocket for later.

'You need any kind of help,' Preacher Man said darkly, 'you give me a call. I decided to stay on here at the Washington for a few more days.' He touched the side of his nose with his index finger. 'I don't have dealings with firearms, but obligation is obligation among friends. Isn't that so?'

Jordan nodded. 'I'll pick you up on that later,' he said

After the funeral, Jordan, Beth and Cary managed to persuade Jordan's mother to return to the Jordan spread. Cary's sisters had come over for the funeral and they decided to stay on at the place for a while to help their mother acclimatize to her grief. Jordan's mother couldn't take in the events of the last few days. She was half demented, not only by the death of her husband, but by the unexpected return of her son Nat after so many years.

'I can't understand how you knew it was time to come home,' she said. 'After all that time too. We thought you were dead, you know.' She stared at him intently for a moment and then stretched out a timorous hand to touch his face. 'This is you, Nathaniel, isn't it? You sure it's you and not a ghost?'

'It's me,' he said. 'And I'm no spook.'

Her lips trembled. 'But why didn't you come back to me sooner, Nat? What kept you away so long? I knew in my heart you were alive and wondered what kept you away.'

Good question. It took Jordan right back to the war again.

After they escaped from the Yankees, Jordan and Coulter managed to get to their own lines again. Coulter was eager to return to the fighting, but Jordan wanted a rest from killing and mayhem.

'I'm going to swing those Yankees right back to

Washington, New York and beyond,' Coulter boasted. He had a strange fire dancing in his eyes, something between determination and valour and the fanaticism of madness.

Jordan had to admire his courage.

So they reported for duty and were drafted into another regiment since most of their comrades had been wiped out after Bull Run.

'Should have taken them then,' Coulter said. 'But those damned generals let everything slip away like sand in the tide. Lee could have prevailed but Davis wouldn't give him a free hand.'

Maybe Jordan should had seen the fanatical streak in him then, but Coulter was given a medal for valour under fire and, on Coulter's recommendation, Jordan was made up to sergeant.

And so they fought on together until Jordan caught a bullet high in his left thigh. A flesh wound, no doubt, but it turned bad and threatened gangrene. In those days when a man got a wound in his arm or leg, the quickest remedy was amputation.

Jordan was lying half-delirious in the hospital tent when he heard the doctors conferring.

'The only thing to do is take that leg off,' one of them said.

'I agree,' another voice replied. 'Leave it much longer gangrene will set in and he'll die. Not a good way to go.'

At that moment Coulter came into the tent. He looked down at Jordan and shook his head. 'How you doing, buddy?' he asked.

Jordan gritted his teeth. 'Be a good idea if you took out your shooter right now and put a ball right through my head.'

Coulter studied the blood-soaked bandages covering the wound. 'What are talking about, you jug-head?'

Jordan rolled his face to one side. 'Doctors say they can't save the leg. They don't have the right disinfectants.'

'Don't talk dumb!' Coulter shouted so loud a soldier in another bed groaned and a nurse came running over and tried to hush Coulter down.

'This brave soldier has to live!' Coulter protested.

A doctor came bustling over. 'We're doing our best, captain, but we can't work miracles here.'

'Miracles be damned!' Coulter raved. 'This sergeant could win this war on his own, one hand tied behind his back! You know that?'

Another doctor appeared. He had the look of authority of a medic in charge. 'I assure you we do our best with what we have,' he said sternly. 'All these brave men deserve to be spared but we can only work with what we've got.'

Coulter was not to be put off. 'Listen up, Doctor!' he said. 'I need this sergeant. The army needs this sergeant. It's your duty to save that leg and keep him alive. You hear me?' There was something in Coulter's eye that Jordan hadn't seen before, and it seemed to impress the two medics. They exchanged uneasy glances and the doctor in charge gave a faint nod.

'We hear you good, Captain, and we understand your concern. Leave it to us and I promise you we'll do our best to get your sergeant on his feet again.'

Coulter walked right up to him and looked him in the face. His eyes seemed to flash out like fire. 'You do better than that,' he said in a low tone. 'You gouge the ball out and save that sergeant's leg. You hear me?'

He patted Jordan on the shoulder solicitously and marched right out of the tent.

Those medics were overstretched and overworked, but they poured spirits on that wound, bound up the leg again and managed to save it. Within days Jordan was in another

77

hospital close to the Rappahannock River being tended by nurses of the Sanitary Commission. That meant learning to walk with crutches, but Jordan was a quick healer and he was soon hopping around the ward and, within a few weeks, he was ready for service again.

They sent him to another unit defending Richmond and he didn't see Coulter again or hear of him . . . until now.

A few days of sunshine. Jordan's mother sat out in the rocking-chair her husband used to sit in, when he wasn't too busy, before he died. That old chair seemed to absorb much of his anger against what he called 'those ornery old-time rebels who can't come to terms with the future of our country!' The old man's cruel death had scattered her brain and she rambled on to herself like a woman half crazed a good deal of the time. But she had her lucid moments. Every time her son's shadow fell between her and the sun she shivered and tensed and thought it was his father come back to haunt her.

'Who's there?' she shouted as Jordan came up the steps.

'It's only me,' Jordan said. 'Your son Nathaniel.'

'Ah, Nathaniel.' She sighed in a moment of clarity. 'Sit down beside me here. I have something particular I wanted to say to you.' She patted the stool beside her.

Jordan put his booted foot on the stool and looked down at his mother. 'What's on your mind, Ma?'

Her eyes came round to scrutinize him sharply and he saw she was lucid again. 'Why are you wearing that belt with the gun, Nathaniel?'

Jordan grinned. 'Never know when you're gonna need a gun. You have to be ready.'

His mother shook her head. 'I see you're troubled, Son, and I know why, sure enough. You feel a deep guilt about your pa's death.'

It was true: Jordan nodded. 'People feel guilty when a man dies. That's why we have funerals.'

His mother didn't question that. She nodded and smiled. 'He was a difficult man,' she croaked, 'but you weren't responsible. That's what I wanted to say to you. Your younger brother Rick has gone to California. Like you, he'll come drifting back one day. Your sisters are more or less fixed. Rosemary has a good husband. And Cary seems happy around the place.' A cloud seemed to pass over her face and she lapsed into a daze, but then she shook her head and revived her thoughts. 'Now you've seen fit to come home, you have to seize your life with both hands.' She made a grabbing motion in the air like she was shaking a rug. 'You got to think about settling down and getting wed. A man needs a partner in this half-tamed country. You know that?'

Jordan scratched his bristly chin. 'I don't think I'm the marrying kind,' he said.

His mother seemed to nod off again, but only for a moment. 'That girl,' she suddenly crowed. 'That girl has had offers from all round. One or two big ranchers through the years, but she turned them all down, you know that?'

'Cary deserves a good husband,' he said.

His mother's eyebrows shot up. 'Who's talking about Cary? You know damned well who I mean. I'm talking about Beth Armitage, you crack-brained idiot!'

That afternoon, close to sundown, Beth rode up to the house with Mex. She dismounted and came up the steps to the porch.

'How's your ma?' she asked Jordan.

Jordan said how his mother seemed to be getting back to her self again. 'Spent time out here in the sunshine for a while. Seemed to do her good. Gave me one of those lectures she specialized in when I was half grown.'

'That's a good sign.' Beth looked into his eyes for a brief moment and then averted her gaze. 'See you got that shooter on,' she said. 'You wear it all the time now?'

'Some time soon, I'm gonna need it,' he said grimly.

Beth sighed and shook her head. 'I'll go along into the house. My ma wants you people to come up to the house for supper tomorrow night. How would that be?'

'Guess that would be fine. I'd appreciate it for the rest of the folks, but I shan't be coming along myself. There's an appointment I've got to keep.'

Beth looked down at the gun at his side and shrugged. 'Suit yourself,' she said.

She went on into the house kind of snooty.

Mex was at the bottom of the steps. Jordan saw him grin darkly under the wide sombrero. 'So you got a rendezvous to keep?' Mex said.

Jordan nodded. 'Tomorrow.'

Mex came up the steps. He was wearing his gunbelt. 'Could be you might need another gun, *amigo*,' he said.

'Could be,' Jordan agreed. 'But could be I have to do this alone.'

Mex nodded. He wasn't a man to push himself forward.

Jordan took the crumpled envelope Preacher Man had given him out of his vest pocket and smoothed the letter. It was written in a good hand like the calligrapher had practised well at school.

'Got this letter third hand through Preacher Man,' he said. 'Don't figure showing it to you in case you get in too deep.'

Mex nodded. 'Seems to me I'm in plenty deep already. A man could drown if he don't know which way to swim.'

Jordan held the letter in the light from the cabin window and read the message:

Sorry your pa had to go. Meet me in the Holdern place between midday and sundown two days after the funeral. Remember, every good rider rides again.
C
Come alone. Otherwise, the deal is off.

He folded the letter and stuck it in the envelope again. 'Like I said, I don't want you in too deep. The message is I should come alone.'

Mex nodded again. 'Could be plumb dangerous on your own. Some kind of wolf jaw you're riding into.'

'That's more than possible,' Jordan agreed. He looked Mex in the eye. 'I've wrastled with wolves before. Happen to know where the Holdern place is?'

Mex considered a moment and then a gleam of intelligence flashed in his eye. 'Sure, I know the Holdern place. Not much of it left now since old man Holdern died. I believe he was killed in a gunfight about five years back in a bar in Redsville. Argument over land rights or something.'

'Could you draw a map, give me directions?' Jordan asked him.

'No big deal,' Mex said. He took a stick and drew a squiggly line in the dust. 'This is the road runs north from Redsville. You keep to it till you come up with a trail that runs off to the left through deep stand of trees. They put up a sign pointing to what was the Holdern place. I believe it's still there. and that's about all I recall.'

'That's good enough,' Jordan said, 'and that's where I might be if I go missing.'

Mex nodded. 'I'll remember that real good.'

At that point the door of the cabin opened and Beth and Cary came out.

'Are you boys having a cosy time out here?' Cary laughed.

'Cosy enough,' Jordan said.

81

CHAPTER SEVEN

Early next day Jordan rode out towards the Holdern place. To get there he had to go through Redsville. He could have skirted round the town but, for some reason he couldn't explain to himself, he rode straight down Main Street past the Washingon Hotel. There was no sign of Preacher Man, or Pike, or anyone else he recognized, but the doors of the Washington were wide open and he saw McGill, the Pinkerton Agent, sitting there with his vest unbuttoned devouring a substantial breakfast. As soon as McGill saw Jordan he got up from the table and came to the door. He beckoned slowly like he was the Angel of Doom and called out something Jordan couldn't catch.

Jordan reined in and dismounted. He tied his horse to the hitching rail and went to meet the portly detective.

'Sorry I missed the funeral,' McGill said with a wry grin. For once he didn't have a fat Havana stuck between his teeth. Maybe smoking cigars and chewing breakfast weren't compatible.

'Not your funeral,' Jordan said. 'So I didn't miss you anyway.'

The detective half offered his hand but Jordan disregarded it.

'So you're riding out,' McGill said.

'Riding somewheres,' Jordan said.

McGill stroked his freshly shaven jaw. 'Thought of pulling out myself. Message came through, I'm needed back in the office in Kansas City. Could be they've got news about the Quantrill bunch.'

His eyes roamed over Jordan and he took in the gunbelt and the Winchester carbine in the sheath at the horse's flank. 'Looks like you're expecting some kind of action yourself. Like I thought, could be you know more than you're telling, Mr Jordan.'

Jordan looked at the Pinkerton man and wondered whether to believe he was going back to Kansas City.

'A man usually knows more than he tells,' he said.

McGill appeared to muse. 'I hear on good authority that friend of yours – Preacher Man, I think he calls himself – got real lathered up last night. Blabbed all over the place before he spewed up his guts. They had to carry him off to his bed and I do believe he lies there still. Chambermaid says how she heard a groaning and a hollering as she went past his door his morning. Could be he'll keep to his bed until sundown.'

'That so?' Jordan said without apparent interest. 'Preacher Man has many gifts. It seems drinking might be one of them.'

McGill squeezed his face into a thoughtful grimace. 'Another thing I heard – that fat incompetent Sheriff Stevenoak has a mind to speak with you. Has some kind of theory about those Quantrill Raiders. I figure it won't amount to a fistful of beans.'

Jordan got ready to mount up. 'Knows where to find me if he wants me,' he said. 'See you around sometime. Maybe here, maybe in Kansas City.'

He unhitched Regius, found the stirrup and swung his leg over the horse's back.

McGill gave a gurgle of mocking laughter. 'My, Mr

Jordan,' he said, 'you begin to resemble a gunman of some renown. Just like you're about to ride out on some holy mission like one of those knights of the round table we hear about in those ancient tales. You should have your portrait done for the family album. So those who come after you can see what you looked like in your prime. You know that?'

Jordan squinted down at the detective from his position high in the saddle. 'Let the future take care of itself, Mr McGill,' he said. 'The present is knocking at the door and we have to let it in or lock it out; either way it won't stay out for long. The longer you try to keep the door shut the bigger and stronger that devil gets.'

The detective opened his mouth in faint surprise. 'That's a good saying, Mr Jordan,' he said. 'I'll have to remember to tell it to my grandchildren.'

'Get your kids first,' Jordan said. 'Don't worry too much on the grandchildren. That's a long ways off.'

Jordan rode on through Redsville and took the rough road that Mex had traced in the dust. The day was fine, though when he looked into the sky he could see from the way the clouds were gathering and mounting up that there might be rain later.

Just as Mex had said there was a signpost a few miles on and it pointed to the Holdern place along a dense and creepy trail. Mex had said by way of a dark wood and there was a dense and knotted thicket ahead. The trail was faint and ill-used, probably hadn't been frequented since old man Holdern was shot to death in that barroom shoot out in Redsville. Gone like those clouds will soon be gone, Jordan thought as he dismounted and turned Regius loose on a promising piece of pasture he had found further along the dingy trail. He sat on a fallen tree with the Winchester across his knees and ate cold chicken and ham, washed

84

down with fresh water from his canteen.

Don't turn now, he thought, you're being watched. A man always senses the presence of others even when he's locked into his own thoughts. He cocked the Winchester across his knees just as the figure stepped out from behind a tree. The *hombre* who had been surveying him was dressed in black and had a black bandanna covering his lower face. He had a six-shooter in his right hand and it was pointing at Jordan.

'You going my way?' the man drawled.

Jordan moved the Winchester round to cover the man. 'Who wants to know?' he enquired.

The man nodded and probably grinned – Jordan couldn't see his mouth so he wasn't sure. 'A lot of people might want to know,' he replied.

A cool customer, Jordan thought. Could probably shoot a man dead without a qualm if he had to.

'Like who for instance?' Jordan asked.

The man nodded slightly again. 'Like the man you're riding to see,' he said.

Each man had his sights on the other. The air in the woodland vibrated and hummed with the sound of insects and another sound that he couldn't quite locate . . . could be the high scream of tension. In the background there was a distant grumble of thunder like a comment from the gods. Though Jordan had his finger on the trigger, ready to squeeze, he figured neither of them intended to fire.

'Why don't you take that bandanna off your face?' Jordan said. 'It doesn't stop me from recognizing you. You're the *hombre* Pike, calls himself Rig. You know it and I know it. So why don't we stop playing games?'

Came a chuckle from behind the bandanna. Pike reached up with his left hand and pulled it down to his neck. While he was distracted Jordan could have shot him

85

clean, but he held his fire.

'So what's the deal?' he asked.

Rig motioned with his shooter. 'You want to meet with Coulter; I take you to meet with Coulter.'

Jordan considered the matter. 'We do have a rendezvous some place,' he said.

'Sure you do,' Pike agreed. 'At the Holdern place, as I recall.' He was standing half concealed behind the gnarled tree from where he had emerged. He could still throw a shot and take cover if he had a mind.

Jordan turned the whole deal over in his mind. 'Some think you're working for the Pinkerton Agency. Leastways, that's what McGill pretends. Maybe he's wrong. Maybe you're working for the Quantrills. Then again, maybe you're working for both sides at once. It has been known.'

Pike stepped from behind the tree with his shooter out straight, pointing directly at Jordan's head. 'That's for you to guess and for me to know.'

Jordan moved his Winchester to get a better bead on the gunman.

'I'm thinking on that one,' he said. 'Just as soon as you lower that Colt pistol and slide it back in its holster I shall be in a better position to work on the answer.'

Pike paused for a moment. Then he uncocked his pistol and stowed it away.

Jordan did the same with his Winchester. He rose from the log and stood facing the man. Pike was lean as a coyote and tough as a hickory branch; in a fight he would be a hard man to fell.

'So, what's the next move?' Jordan asked.

'The next move is you ride along with me. I take you to your rendezvous and you parley with the boss man.'

Jordan gathered in Regius, slid the carbine into its sheath, and mounted up. Pike had retrieved his own horse, and they rode on together through the darkening wood. Into the jaws of death, Jordan thought.

It was a long ride through broken country. A man could search for ever and a day without encountering the Quantrill bunch. As they rode, Jordan could hear the rumble of thunder drawing closer. The coming storm could ride out over the plains, or sweep in through the woodlands where they were jogging on obliviously.

Jordan kept Pike on his right, not too close. Though the gunman watched him from under his dark hat, he kept his hand away from the Colt. Even a gunman has to have a reason to kill, Jordan figured, and this man Pike has been told to bring me in alive.

When the storm came sweeping in, it blew hard on the trees and the two riders paused to shelter in a convenient cave. Rig seemed to know the lie of the land. Jordan took particular note of that. As they sheltered, stirrup to stirrup under the rocks, Rig rolled himself a quirly and started to smoke.

'You want me to roll you one?' he asked.

'Don't use them,' Jordan said. 'How far do we go?'

Rig held up his quirly and studied it thoughtfully. 'Not so far. We get there by sundown.'

As soon as the rain passed over, Rig spurred his mount on and Jordan followed on Regius.

'Good piece of horseflesh, you got there,' Pike remarked. The only sociable comment that passed between them.

Like Pike said, it was sundown when they reached their destination. Pike gave a high-pitched whistle and an answer came back immediately. Jordan saw the flames of a fire dancing among the trees. Behind it, vaguely outlined, was the shape of a cabin or shack. At the fire a man in a long, caped waterproof sat roasting a jack-rabbit on a stick. Jordan knew even before he looked up that it was Coulter.

'You reeled him in?' Coulter said.

Pike nodded. 'Real quiet fish,' he said.

Coulter rose from the fire and laid the carcass on an iron griddle.

'So you came, Sergeant,' he said to Jordan.

'Got your note,' Jordan said as he swung down from Regius.

'Seems you got your leg back OK,' Coulter observed as Jordan stood beside the horse.

'I got it good thanks to you, Captain,' Jordan said.

Coulter turned to Pike and gave a flick of his hand. 'OK, Soldier. The sergeant and I need to talk.'

Pike hesitated a moment. Then he turned his horse away and rode off into the darkness.

Coulter sat down again and held the jack-rabbit to the fire again. 'Weren't sure you'd come,' he said. 'Sit down and have a bite.'

Jordan released Regius and sat down on a log facing Coulter across the fire. He could have drawn his Colt and shot Coulter right between the eyes if he'd wanted to.

'Just like old times,' Coulter remarked. 'You and me in the woods behind enemy lines. You remember that?'

Jordan did remember vividly. He thought of a time when they had had to abandon the carcass of a deer and run for their lives. Now they were sitting beside a fire with the woods all round them, apparently alone, though there were flickers of light accompanied by muffled voices from the abandoned shack. So they weren't quite alone; Jordan knew that. Those raiders were all around camping in the woods, fifteen, maybe twenty of them or more, he figured.

'So we have a choice here,' Coulter said, as they chewed

88

on their meal. 'A question of whether you ride with me or not.'

Jordan dislodged a piece of bone in his mouth and spat it into the fire. There was a quick hissing sound like derision.

'You killed my pa,' he announced slowly.

Coulter showed no surprise. He swallowed hard and stared at the dancing flames for a while. Then he cleared his throat. 'That was a bad deal,' he admitted, 'but it had to be done. Fortunes of war. You know that and I know that.' He looked up quickly and fixed a steady unrelenting gaze on Jordan. 'Men on opposite sides of the fence. There's a time to die and a time to kill.'

'Tell me about it,' Jordan said.

Now a faint expression of uneasiness passed over Coulter's face. 'You know we're in a war here,' he said. 'Your old man was the enemy. He knew what was coming to him and he faced it like a man. I have to admire him for that.'

Jordan considered the notion, apparently without emotion, for a while.

'You went to an old man's home and you strung him up in his own living-room,' he said. 'You locked my ma and my sister in the barn and then strung up the old man. War or peace, what can anyone gain from an action like that?'

Coulter swallowed again and then leaned forward. The flames of the fire danced in his eyes like he was a devil from one of the deep circles of Hell.

'Some say the war ended and the Confederate forces were defeated,' he said, 'but you and I know different. We weren't defeated. We were betrayed by Jefferson Davis and all those crook generals. If we'd kept our nerve, we could have taken Washington and put Lincoln against the wall and shot him. That's why William Quantrill lives on.'

Jordan was still chewing though he felt like spitting the rest of the rabbit onto the fire. 'Quantrill is dead,' he said.

'Killed by the Union back in '65.'

Coulter gave a deep sceptical laugh. 'That's what they say and that's what you believe.' He leaned forward over the fire. 'I tell you Quantrill's alive. He's teaching school down in Texas. He's just biding his time. Soon as he's ready, he's coming back to join us. Together we're gonna sweep away the past and bring on the future . . . restore this country to what it should be.'

Jordan was silent for a moment; then he spoke in a very level tone. 'My pa swung there from a beam choking his life out,' he repeated.

Coulter went on without flinching. 'We gave your old man a trial and pronounced sentence,' he said. 'He knew what to expect and he accepted it like a man.'

Coulter got to his feet and stood like a latter-day Napoleon. 'And you,' he said, 'you were once a damned good Confederate soldier, Jordan. Now, I throw you a challenge. I want you to join me and help me to restore things as they used to be and as they should be. I have to ask you this question: are you for us or against us?'

Jordan considered for a moment and then rose slowly from the fire.

There was a moment of absolute quiet except for the crackle and hiss of the flames and the intense breathing of the two men. Jordan could have drawn his weapon and shot Coulter right through the heart where he stood. Coulter had a shooter in a holster strapped to his thigh. He could have drawn too and taken a shot at his old sergeant. But neither moved.

'What's your choice?' Coulter demanded.

Jordan shook his head. 'My choice is this, Captain: I'm riding out now. If we meet again I'll shoot you down. That's my choice.'

At that moment Jordan knew that Coulter was mad . . .

mad as a rabid dog! You have to shoot a rabid dog. Yet he
turned slowly and gave a whistle. Regius was a pace or two
away. Yet, before Jordan swung his leg over the horse's back,
the madman could have drawn and thrown a shot at him
and brought him down.

When he was in the saddle, in the moment before he
broke away, he knew that he was fully exposed to the fury of
his old captain. But Coulter remained standing with an
expression of astonishment and fanatical fury on his face.

Jordan wheeled his horse and rode away through the
trees.

As he rode, he was aware of shadowy forms rising in the
distance and circling towards him through the thicket:
Coulter's men, he knew, among them possibly the man Pike
who had guided him in. You damned fool, he thought. You
could have killed Coulter stone dead with a single shot. You
could have torn this mad rebellion out by its twisted roots
and stamped it dead! And what do you do? You leave yourself exposed on every side to a bunch of mad killers who
killed your pa. You've put your foot in a hornets' nest and
you're about to get stung and stung and stung again . . . to
death!

Yet, as he rode, he recalled the hospital where he had
lain with his gashed leg and the moment when Captain
Coulter had leaned over and raved at those medics: *you
gouge that ball out and save that sergeant's leg. You hear me!.*
They had saved that leg and that was why he was riding now
through the trees looking for the trail where he could
gallop free. Regius was a damned good piece of horseflesh
and when they reached level ground he would go like a bolt
out of hell.

But those Quantrill Raiders were already gaining ground
and riding close. Jordan could hear the sound of their hoofs

pounding the ground, getting nearer every second. He turned in the saddle and saw a particularly determined *hombre* riding like a phantom between the trees, gun held high looking for a clear point where he could throw a shot.

Suddenly the woods cleared and Regius was galloping into open country. Jordan's pursuer took a bead on Jordan and fired a couple of shots. The first went wide, the second whined in so close Jordan felt its hot breath on his cheek. He swung in the saddle and took a quick shot at his pursuer. It missed. Difficult to bring down a man from a galloping horse.

Take a chance. Jordan reined in and turned. His pursuer was struggling to bring his horse under control. Jordan saw him struggling with the reins in the light of the rising moon. He took a bead on the rider and fired. His pursuer's horse reared. The man raised his gun to shoot, and then slid sideways in the saddle and fell.

Regius was prancing and neighing like he was desperate to get going. You beauty! Jordan thought. You damned fine beauty. That Indian who sold me this horse sure knew what he was doing. Preacher Man, too. He knew his trade!

Jordan paused to listen. No sound except for the soughing of the wind through the upper branches. He rode on through low scrub onto an area of undulating prairie, making a detour away from the wood and in the opposite direction from Redsville. Those Quantrill Raiders could fan out and hunt him down, but that wouldn't be easy even in the light of the rising moon.

So he stopped to give Regius a blow. There was a little dip in the prairie where he could stand and fight. He drew in close beside a thicket of willows by a pool, and waited with the Winchester cocked and ready. A good position to see off towards the woods from where he had ridden.

He could hear them coming, a whole bunch of riders

but not as many as a score . . . maybe ten. They came riding together through the pale moonlight, searching every which way like a crowd of jabbering blind men. Moonlight can help a man to see but it can also help a man to hide.

The riders paused in a crowd to parley. He could hear them talking and almost distinguish the words. Their tone told him they didn't know which way to search. Someone gave a command and they spurred away in a bunch like a troop of cavalrymen uncertain where to find their enemy.

All but two. As the others rode off, two riders stood and conferred. Then he tightened his grip on Winchester and spoke quiet words of reassurance to Regius. Time to kill, he thought, as the two riders came straight towards him.

They paused close by the edge of the pool and peered across. Jordan put his hand on Regius's nose to keep him quiet. The horse seemed to catch the mood. He tossed his head and kept himself still.

'Could be somewheres in there,' one of the riders murmured.

'Could be anywhere,' the other replied dubiously.

'Maybe we should go in for a looksee.'

The second *hombre* didn't seem too keen on the sugges-tion. It was dark under the trees and, if someone was wait-ing there in the gloom, he could see them and they would-n't see him so easily. A good shootist could pick them off as easily as shooting clay pigeons at a fair.

As if to emphasize this, the moon passed behind a loud and the hollow was thrown into impenetrable shade.

'Let's get going,' he first rider said. 'We're wasting our time here. Could be anywheres.'

The two riders backed away from the hollow and rode off. Jordan could still hear the rest of the bunch rousting around on the prairie. He patted Regius on the neck and murmured a word of thanks, directed more at himself than the horse.

When the sounds had died away and the moon had reappeared from behind the cloud, he rode onto the prairie and circled round in the direction of Redsville.

No more sounds of pursuit. The night was quiet and peaceful. He rode on without haste under a moon like a silver plate. Should he count his chickens? He wasn't sure. The war had hardened him and made him pessimistic. Maybe he should have taken his chance and shot Coulter as he sat beside the fire. He figured Coulter could have blown his brains out as he mounted Regius to ride away. A strange *hombre*! Though they had ridden together like brothers, Coulter had always kept himself partly hidden. Probably a question of rank, but it was more than that. Now, after so many years, Jordan suddenly saw the full dimension of the man – a man who could have another man lynched simply because of what he said. In his memory Jordan saw Coulter crouching like a demon roasting a rabbit on a stick. The picture had a symbolism about it that Jordan couldn't quite figure.

He reached the trail and rode on towards the Holdern place . . . or what was left of it. A sombre shack with a sign hanging under the buffalo skull by the drive-in. The shack was leaning to one side like you could have pushed it over if you leaned on it too hard. It was covered with green tendrils and moss as though nature had got a deadly grip on it and was slowly strangling it.

As Jordan rode up to the place, he sensed that something or someone was waiting for him in the blackness under the lintel.

'So,' a voice said, 'you got yourself away from Captain Coulter then, did you?'

94

'I didn't go much on what he said,' Jordan replied.

Pike chuckled quietly under the lintel. 'That's the way it is with Coulter. Either you're with him or you're against him. No half measures with Captain Coulter.'

'So I guess you're with him,' Jordan speculated.

There was a moment's silence as Pike turned the proposition over in his mind. 'Could be,' he said from the darkness. 'Then again, might not be. Life has complications. But I guess you know that.'

Regius stirred and Jordan took the point.

'So that's why you're waiting here to escort me home,' he said.

Pike gave another sombre chuckle in the darkness. 'That could be so,' he said. 'You could say I'm your reception committee, or your execution squad. Maybe you'll never know which.'

Jordan heard the faint click of Pike's Colt and knew he was about to fire. He threw himself sideways off Regius's back. As he did so he saw the flash in the doorway. He rolled over and over behind the fence. Regius whinnied and reared – a welcome distraction. Jordan bunched up against a post and drew his Colt. He threw a shot at the black space from where he had seen the flash.

But Pike was nobody's fool. He didn't figure to keep himself in the dark frame of the doorway and get himself cut down. He sprang sideways among creepers and branches as Jordan cocked his pistol.

'You're making a big mistake here,' Pike breathed hoarsely.

'That what you figure?' Jordan said. Now he was on his knees behind a fence post waiting for Pike to show his position.

Pike made a sound that was more of a growl than a chuckle. 'It was real dumb to ride back the way you went in,' he said. 'The Holdern place has a curse on it like Holdern himself. That big horse of yours senses that. That's why he reared up and made to gallop off. Doesn't care for ghouls and ghosts and stuff.'

Jordan was listening and waiting. He hadn't figured Pike for much of a talking *hombre*. Ashes thrown in a man's eyes. He knew the gunman was working for a better position from where he could shoot him down.

'Tell you what,' Pike said, 'Why don't we call a truce? Honour satisfied. We can postpone the execution till later. How would that be?'

Jordan gave a brief laugh. 'And I have another suggestion,' he said. 'You throw out that shooter of yours and come out of those shadows with your hands above your head, I might consider that proposition and treat you nice.'

There was a moment's silence. Reluctance or cunning? 'OK, we have a deal here,' Pike said. 'You step away from that fence and stow your shooter. I throw out my shooter. Then we both back off. You go your way: I go my way. That's the deal.'

'Throw out your shooter,' Jordan said.

Another pause. Then an object was thrown out of the shadows and clattered on the stones.

Jordan rose cautiously and backed away.

Pike came out of the darkness, but not with his hands raised. He came with guns blazing! Bam! Bam!

Jordan steadied himself and loosed off a single shot.

Pike came blundering and roaring on towards him. The gunman fired just one more shot. Then he pitched forward onto his face.

Jordan could still hear Pike's harsh breath escaping. Could be a trick, or could be a death rattle.

He went forward and put his gun against Pike's head.

Pike stirred. He made one last supreme effort to pull

himself up and raise his shooter. The moon rose from behind a trail of cloud to watch.

'You killed me!' Pike gasped. 'You damned killed me!'

He gave a last sigh and fell forward on his face.

CHAPTER EIGHT

The Washington was ablaze with light. As he rode into Redsville he saw through the lemon-tinted windows the figures of dancing men and women moving and gesticulating like puppets. As he drew close, he could hear the sound of Preacher Man's fiddle scraping away like he was trying to saw through a whole pile of logs. The fiddler had obviously recovered from his roistering the night before and was in excellent form.

Jordan passed by and drew up beside the funeral parlour run by Jonathan Fawcett. Though it was late he saw the square shape of Jonathan planing away at a plank of wood. Already working on a good coffin for a man called Pike, he thought.

Jordan dismounted and hitched the two horses to the hitching rail. He stood in the doorway and looked at the burly coffin maker.

'Evening, Jonathan,' he said.

Fawcett looked up over the coffin he was planing and his hair almost stood up like corn stalks. 'My Gawd, Jordan, You got blood on your face. You look like a ghost!'

It was the first time Jordan had thought about his appearance since Pike had died in front of the Holdern place.

'I am a ghost, pretty much,' he said. 'I brought you a customer for that coffin you're making.'

Fawcett went to the door and looked out and saw the body of Pike hanging over his horse's back. 'You kill this man?' he asked warily.

'Self-defence,' Jordan said. 'He tried to gun me down .'

Fawcett shook his head slowly. 'Tell that to the judge,' he said. 'This here's a Pinkerton man. You killed him you've got a deal of explaining to do.'

'That's what I intend,' Jordan said. 'Pike was no Pinkerton man unless the agency is working with the Quantrill bunch.'

'Well, I'll be damned!' Fawcett exclaimed.

Talking of the judge, Jordan didn't have long to wait. Despite the dancing and raving in the Washington, inquisitive eyes had seen the man riding through town trailing a horse with a corpse across it. Eager faces peered in through Jonathan Fawcett's window and in a matter of seconds the huge form of Sheriff Stevenoak came rubbing away sleep from his eyes.

'What's this?' he enquired. 'It seems a man is dead here. Who brought him in?'

'Tried to shoot me: I had to kill him in self-defence,' Jordan explained.

Stevenoak stood with his thumbs in his suspenders, a man who liked showing off to a responsive audience, but, as McGill had said, not a man of real resolution and courage. Jordan tried to tell him what had happened. When he got to the part where Coulter was sitting by the fire, he saw the look of wariness and suspicion cross the sheriff's face.

'You mean you talked to Coulter?' he asked in astonishment.

Jordan searched through his pockets for Coulter's letter, but it seemed to be missing. A look of settled perplexity crossed the sheriff's pear-shaped face. 'I don't figure this,' he said. 'I guess you know this man Pike, who calls himself Rig, was working for Mr McGill, the Pinkerton agent. How could a Pinkerton agent be one of the Quantrill mob? That don't make no sense to me.'

Jordan shrugged. 'I guess you need to ask McGill and Coulter about that,' he said.

The faces of the crowd were pressing in close. Stevenoak might have appreciated an audience but he liked to be on firm ground. 'Now, Mr Jordan,' he said cautiously, 'we got to get to the bottom of this before it gets way out of hand.' He pulled himself up and swelled out to show his sheriff's badge and give himself gravitas. 'This is a matter for the judge. I'm going to have to ask you to hand in your weapon and give yourself up so we can get to the truth about this whole sorry business.'

Jordan considered the matter. 'When is the judge due in?'

Stevenoak looked thoughtful. 'I do believe Judge Winter is coming next week. Yes, that's right: he's coming beginning of next week. I send him a wire, he'll be here.'

Jordan was thinking things over. It seemed he could either make a break for it or surrender himself to the sheriff and hope for a fair outcome. There seemed no other way. He shrugged. 'Maybe we should walk down to your office and talk this through.'

Stevenoak nodded ponderously.

They carried Pike's body through the workshop and laid it face-up on a broad pine table. Pike had not been exactly handsome but now his features had relaxed into a kind of peacefulness . . . not quite angelic, but not exactly the ugly face of a killer either. There was a single wound under his heart and surprisingly little blood.

'Looks kind of saintly, don't he?' Stevenoak reflected. Not the most tactful thing to say. Stevenoak was not the brightest of lawmen but he knew procedure. He collected Pike's weapons and sniffed at them suspiciously. He looked at the chambers with an air of judicial importance. 'Two shells left. Seems he fired four shots.'

'He took four shots at me,' Jordan confirmed.

'And you shot him clean through the chest – a single shot!' Stevenoak said in some surprise.

'I fired two shots,' Jordan affirmed.

Jonathan Fawcett took charge of the horses and Jordan and Stevenoak walked down to the jail. He made as if to put his hand on Jordan's shoulder but Jordan shook it off like it was a troublesome fly. Stevenoak decided not to make an issue of the matter and they walked on down Main Street trailing a swelling bunch of curious citizens.

Stevenoak hadn't taken Jordan's Colt and Jordan could have held him up and made a break, but he was turning matters over in his mind. Among other things he was thinking about Coulter and which way his old buddy might jump. He was also thinking of Beth and his mother and sister and what might happen to them if there was nobody to take care of them.

Stevenoak cranked back the cell door. 'Now I'm going to ask you to give up your gun, Mr Jordan,' he said nervously. 'Judge Winter will need it for evidence.'

Jordan unbuckled his gunbelt and handed it over. He went into the cell and tested the springs of the bed as Stevenoak turned the key.

He didn't sleep like a babe, but it had been a long day and he dreamt of Captain Coulter roasting a rabbit over a fire. He woke with a start and saw a vision of a man in a black bowler wearing a bow tie and matching waistcoat. It took him a second or two to recognize Preacher Man.

'Hi there, partner,' the fiddler said. 'Seems you got yourself a deal of trouble. I supervised your breakfast and had it brought in. Ham and eggs if that's OK. Probably hash browns too. They're real sorry the way things turned out at the Washington. McGill too. He don't seem too pleased about that man Pike you shot. You have a lot of explaining to do and that's a fact.'

'Man turns a gun on you, you don't ask questions; you shoot first and then speak,' Jordan said.

'At least you managed to preserve that noble beast I got for you,' Preacher Man said. 'I walked down soon as I heard. They're looking after him real good in the livery stable.' He leaned in close to the bars. 'My guess is you're gonna need that horse soon. Got to keep him in good shape.' He gave a slow full wink.

Jordan didn't wink back. He could see Stevenoak fussing around in the background, probably trying to pick up on the conversation.

'So McGill is still in town,' Jordan speculated. 'He talked about going back to Kansas City.'

Preacher Man lowered his voice. 'Rumour has it, he sensed the possibility of a shift in the wind direction. Thought it better to stick around.'

Stevenoak was whistling to himself in the office. He was cleaning and oiling his stock of weapons. Probably preening himself for making such an easy arrest, Jordan thought as he did press ups against the bars of his cell.

Jordan's next visitor came around midday. Predictably it was McGill, the Pinkerton agent.

McGill stood in the doorway of the office, sucking on a Havana and consulting his gold timepiece.

'So you shot my man Pike,' he boomed out through the office.

Jordan sat on the none-too-comfortable cot and waited for the agent to come close to the bars.

McGill raised his hands and gripped the bars. 'Got yourself in a real fix here, Jordan. You know that?' He sounded angry underneath the pretended good humour.

Jordan rose from the cot slowly. 'A man kills another man he has some explaining to do,' he said. 'A man who employs a gunman and lets him gun down an enquiring stranger has a deal more explaining to do.'

McGill chewed his cigar thoughtfully. He took the cigar out of his mouth, examined it critically, and spat out a speck of tobacco into the cell. 'You want to tell me what happened, Mr Jordan?' he asked.

Jordan moved his head slowly from side to side. 'Maybe I should save that for Judge Winter. Sheriff Stevenoak tells me he's rolling in next week.'

McGill moved the cigar from one side of his mouth to the other. He puffed out a small ring of blue-grey smoke. 'I'm trying to figure this,' he drawled. 'This man Pike you killed was with me five years or more. Very reliable too. Never had a pinch of trouble from him.'

'So you didn't know he was a double-crosser?' Jordan said. 'Working for you and the opposition at the same time?'

McGill speculated a little further. 'Could be another version of that,' he said. 'Could be you're in with the Quantrills yourself. After all, you shed good red blood for the Confederate cause. Could be my man Pike was following a lead. You knew he had the goods on you. So you took him out.' McGill grinned to himself. 'Least that's what the stars could be saying.'

Jordan nodded grimly. 'Those stars could be saying bull-shit, Mr McGill,' he said. 'You know that and I know that.'

'That case,' McGill said, 'I'd better consult the tea leaves next time.'

As he turned away, Jordan saw the Colt riding high on his hip.

*

Stevenoak had apparently been listening in on this conversation . . . listening and making notes in a note-book he kept. Though he wasn't exactly a thinking man, he could read and write and he prided himself on the copious reports he made when Judge Winter was coming to town.

As Jordan wondered how long he could stay cooped up in this hell hole, two horses arrived and their riders came into the office. One was Mex and the other was Beth. Mex had a grim look of determination on his face and Beth threw Jordan a smile that warmed him like no fire he had ever experienced. She turned to Sheriff Stevenoak.

'Why have you got Nathaniel Jordan caged up like this?' she demanded.

Stevenoak blushed with bewilderment. He had always had a shine for Beth, hoped once she might agree to jump the lariat with him. 'I don't mean to, Miss Beth,' he said. 'It's a question of evidence. Mr Jordan shot that man Pike dead. He admits it himself. Brought Pike's body in on his horse's back last night. Claims it was self-defence, but a death is a death and the law has to look into it. Everybody knows that.' By the end of his explanation Stevenoak was stumbling over his words and wringing his hands together like he had blotted his copy book at school.

But Beth was not a woman to be put off. 'That may be so,' she insisted, 'but I want Mr Jordan out on bail. I'll stand surety if necessary. You name the price and I'll give my word he'll come in next week to face Judge Winter.'

That made Jordan feel like an unclaimed parcel in a postal depot; he was surprised and embarrassed by Beth's determination on his behalf.

Stevenoak looked up at the office ceiling and dithered. For a moment his shine for Beth and his position as sheriff were locked in close combat together. Then he bit his lip. 'Can't do that, Miss Beth. I'm a sheriff of the law. I'm afraid Mr Jordan has to stay right where he is until the judge comes.'

Beth looked him right in the eye until he had to look away. 'Very well, then,' she said. 'Just so long as you let me and Mex go into the cell with him so we can talk.'

Stevenoak considered that reasonable. He shrugged his heavy shoulders. 'I shouldn't be doing this, Miss Beth,' he said. 'Fact, I wouldn't for nobody else.' He took the key to the cell off the hook at the back of his desk and opened the door of Jordan's cell.

Beth went inside. Jordan's arms went round her of their own accord just like that was the natural place for them.

Mex made a move towards the cell and Stevenoak put out a hand to restrain him. 'Before you go in that cell, Mex, I must trouble you to take off that artillery you got on your hip and hand it over. Can't have a man going into a cell with a forty-five on his belt. It's against the law.'

Mex gave the sheriff a cool look. He unbuckled his gunbelt and held it dangling under the sheriff's nose.

'Sorry I have to do this,' the sheriff said. He took the belt and slid it into a drawer in his desk.

A half-hour later Beth came to the cell door and rattled the bars. 'OK, you can let us out now, Mr Stevenoak.'

Stevenoak had taken the precaution of locking the three of them in the cell. Now he took the key and unlocked the door. Mex and Beth came out, looking somewhat thoughtful. Jordan stood just inside the cell.

'I have a proposition to put before you,' he said to Stevenoak.

The sheriff darted a wary look at him. 'What proposition is that?' he asked suspiciously.

'Just this,' Jordan said. 'You questioned me last night and I told you the truth. My proposition is this: we ride out together and check on the evidence. First we go to the Holdern place and take a mosey around. Then we ride on to where I rendezvoused with Coulter and have a look see. Could find something interesting. Then you might believe I'm telling you the truth about Pike and Coulter.'

Stevenoak rubbed his chin. 'I didn't say I didn't believe you, Mr Jordan,' he said. 'The law has to be suspicious. That's why it must go before the judge.' He shrugged his shoulders and glanced at Mex. 'We ride out there – and I don't say you ain't telling me the way it happened – how do I know you might not try to gun down on me? Could be you're just leading me out there by the nose so that Coulter and those Quantrill Raiders could do something to humble the law, or hold me hostage or something?'

Beth spoke up again. 'Mr Stevenoak, you can put your mind at rest on that. If you agree to ride out with us, I can guarantee you'll ride back again . . . unless something unaccountable happens.'

A look of nervous apprehension clouded the sheriff's face. Then he looked at her with a new light in his eye. 'You suggesting we all ride together?' he asked thoughtfully. 'You, me, Jordan and Mex?'

'That's what I'm suggesting, Mr Stevenoak,' she said.

Stevenoak kept stroking his chin thoughtfully. He looked at Beth, then at Mex, and finally at Jordan who was still standing in the cell. 'I don't see what there is to gain by this,' he ruminated.

Jordan shrugged. 'We have a whole lot to gain,' he said. He took a deep breath. 'These so-called Quantrill Raiders mean to wreak havoc on the whole country. We know that from the way they killed my pa because he spoke out in favour of the Unionist cause. Those crazy men mean to start the whole cycle of war again.'

Stevenoak stopped playing with his jaw and looked up sharply at Jordan. 'That could be true,' he admitted.

'Damned right it's true!' Jordan said fervently. 'I know Coulter. We rode together. He saved my life more than once. He saved my leg when those medics were set to remove it. I know what Coulter's capable of. We ride out now and find out where that bunch is, we could do something to stop them before they kill a lot more people and do a lot more damage.'

That swung it. Stevenoak suddenly stuck out the star of authority on his chest. 'Do I have your word you won't cheat me in this?' he asked.

Jordan nodded. 'If that means anything to you, you have my word.'

Beth went down to the livery stable to redeem Regius and the others assembled behind the jail. Stevenoak figured it wasn't wise to draw too much attention to themselves. They rode out at an angle from Redsville and circled back towards the trail that led in the direction of the Holdern place.

Now that Stevenoak had fallen in with the idea of verifying Jordan's story he became puffed up with enthusiasm like he had thought up the whole idea himself. The rest of them said little. Jordan was worried about Beth. More and more he realized that that the girl had real sand. As they rode close together their knees collided gently, but, although the blood raced in their veins, neither gave a sign Mex rode slightly behind, glancing warily off to right and left. Though he hadn't been in the recent war, he knew how to look after himself and those he was with like a true soldier.

When they approached the Holdern place, Mex rode

ahead and raised his hand. They stopped a little short of the place.

It looked different in daylight but scarcely less sinister.

Mex dismounted and went forward to reconstruct the events. 'The gunman was waiting here under the ramada,' he said. 'He threw two shots at you and moved out there so he wasn't framed in the doorway?'

Jordan nodded. He was still in the saddle, trying to remember the details.

Mex moved down towards the dilapidated fence. 'This where you were when you fired back at him?'

'That's the spot,' Jordan agreed. He remembered crouching behind the post, pumping one off at the gunman.

'Then he came out of cover and ran towards you,' Mex said.

'That's when I stopped him,' Jordan said.

Mex was still crouching by the post, looking towards the broken-down shack.

'Why did that *hombre* bushwhack you like that?' Stevenoak asked.

'Coulter sent him ahead to gun me down,' Jordan suggested. 'Only thing I can think off.'

'To gun down on his old buddy?' Stevenoak grinned incredulously.

'It happens,' Jordan said. 'Didn't some wise guy say "all's fair in love and war"? Coulter thinks this is war.'

That seemed to impress Stevenoak. He opened his mouth to say something, but Mex got in first. He was on his feet holding a crumpled sheet of paper. 'This proves something.' He rose and held it out to Jordan.

Jordan took the paper and read the message out loud:

Sorry your pa had to go. Meet me in the Holdern place

between midday and sundown two days after the funeral.
Remember, every good rider rides again.
C
Come alone. Otherwise, the deal is off.

Jordan handed the paper to the sheriff. 'Must have come out of my pants pocket just before I took that shot at Pike,' he said.

Stevenoak looked at the paper for almost a minute, trying to figure out exactly what it meant.

'Now we ride on,' Jordan suggested. 'I show you where I came up with Coulter at that damned camp-fire.'

Nobody objected. So Mex mounted up and they rode on again.

CHAPTER NINE

Stevenoak was thinking which accounted for the way he rode, head down, looking at the ground. The sheriff wasn't a great thinker and he couldn't quite figure what his next move should be.

Jordan led the way along the trail that went on past the Holdern's place. He was thinking too, hoping he could find the right way into the close woodland where he had met Coulter squatting by the fire with the jack-rabbit. The land looked a deal different in daylight from when you had last seen it in the sheen of a moon. He had ridden these trails a while back when he was a boy. Even recalled the Holdern place when old man Holdern had constructed the cabin out of raw timber as Mex had described it. He looked out over the prairie which seemed to undulate more than he remembered. Where was the stand of willows where he had hidden himself while the raiders rode by and the two men had detached themselves from the bunch to look for him in the dense shadows? Exactly how long had he ridden to escape from the bunch? He couldn't be certain.

Mex was searching diligently along the edge of the forest. He suddenly reined in and caught at a branch.

'This is likely where you came out of the woods,' he said solemnly. 'Those tracks over there are where the raiders came after you and these tracks here are your horse's tracks, sure enough.'

Jordan stood up in the stirrups and peered out over the prairie. In the distance he saw what looked like the stand of trees where he had waited with his hand over Regius's muzzle to keep him quiet. But there were other stands too and other scrubby areas where he might have hidden.

He turned Regius and sidled towards the wood. Yes, this must be where he had burst out onto the range. Just a broken branch you might overlook and some hoof marks dug into the damp ground. Somewhere in among those trees the pursuer he had shot down must be lying dead.

He led the way among the trees more hopefully with Mex beside him, searching along the ground for hoof marks and signs. Luckily it had rained the night before and the ground was soft.

Even before they came to the spot where Coulter had been waiting for him by the fire, the sound of eerie music came to their ears. Someone was singing in a weird unnerving voice.

A grave in the wood with grass o'ergrown.
A grave in the heart of his mother.
His clay in the one, lifeless and lone,
But his memory lives in another.

The voice of the man singing came out rich and wavery between the trees. The four riders reined in their horses as if by mutual agreement and sat listening uneasily. Stevenoak's pear-shaped face looked startled and terrified.

'My gawd, this place is danged witched!' he murmured.

Beth and Jordan glanced at one another apprehensively. Only Mex registered no emotion.

Jordan urged his mount forward and came to the place.

111

This was where Coulter had sat roasting the rabbit and looking like the devil out of hell, but Coulter had gone. Now another man was sitting in the same position. He wasn't cooking; he was singing in a wavering half-crazy voice. He wore a wide floppy hat all greased up with a bunch of feathers sprouting from it. His grey hair reached down over his shoulders and spread out like the hair of an old woman who had never seen a comb. As the four riders approached and looked down at him, his eyes swivelled to focus on them but he showed no particular concern.

Stevenoak's jaw hung down in astonishment, and the others stood waiting as the old man continued to sing.

He took his time. He sang a verse and went into the chorus again, pleasing himself. He took out a mouth organ and wiped it on his tattered jeans ready to play. Then he looked up at Jordan.

'You come far, mister?' he asked.

Jordan paused. 'Come from Redsville,' he said.

The old man nodded. 'Make yourself welcome. Ain't got much so can't give you much.'

Jordan and Stevenoak dismounted. Stevenoak still looked as though he'd stumbled on a land of fairies and witches.

'You been setting here long?' he asked warily.

The old-timer tapped the mouth organ on his knee again and examined it thoughtfully. 'Been here since time began,' he crowed. 'Live in that shack squatting among the trees yonder. Sometimes think I ought to move before they find me setting here stiff and dead before the fire.'

Jordan looked towards the shack which had appeared nothing but a jumble of shadows the night before. 'You mean you were here last night?' he asked.

'Nope,' the old man said. 'I was setting over yonder in my shack. It ain't much but I count it as home even when the

rain leaks in.' He guffawed in a low creaky voice. He practised a few thin notes on his mouth organ and jabbed the
instrument at Jordan. 'I seed you, mister. My eyes may be
dim but I remember you. I was setting there in the dark
when you rode in with that other man. I heared you talking
to Captain Coulter. Then you broke off the parley real
sudden and rode away. That was a quick move. You got a
fine piece of horse flesh there. That there caused a deal of
ruckus. Those Quantrills that's what they call themselves –
most of them lit out after you like they was a swarm of
hornets.' He took in a breath and peered up at Jordan with
one eye closed. 'That was you, mister, I guess. You must have
got clean away otherwise you wouldn't here. Lucky you got
that good horse of yourn.' He paused again to reach for a
coffee pot on a stone close by the fire. 'Ain't got much but
maybe you'll take a mug of Arbuckle with me. Show there
ain't no hard feelings an' all.'

Jordan sat a little off from the old-timer on a log.
Stevenoak peered about warily, uncertain how to act. Beth
dismounted and took another log for a seat. Mex didn't
seem inclined to dismount. He urged his horse on and rode
towards the shack which leaned on one side like it was a
man who had taken too many drinks for his own good.

'You won't find nothing in there,' the old man called
over his shoulder. 'There ain't nothing to find. Those
Quantrill boys cleaned me out. Not that there was much to
clean out.' He guffawed again.

Jordan accepted a mug of coffee, took a swig, and
handed it on to Beth. It tasted bitter and strong and had a
kick like a buffalo.

'So you know Coulter and those riders who came here
last night?' Jordan said.

The old man gave him a suspicious glance. 'I know them,
mister, but I ain't telling you nothing.'

113

'You realize those men are killers?' Stevenoak piped up suddenly.

The old man gave Stevenoak a quizzical glance. 'You the sheriff?' he demanded.

Stevenoak nodded. 'I'm Sheriff of Redsville.'

The old man shook his head. 'Your authority don't reach as far as this. Sheriff don't mean nothing out here. If'n you're looking for those Quantrills you can stop wasting your time cause they've gorn.'

Stevenoak shook his head. 'You say you're familiar with those raiders?' he asked needlessly.

'Told you I knowed them, didn't I?' the old man complained. 'But I ain't saying nothing to you. They never did me no harm and I ain't doing them no harm.'

'You ever seen that man Pike or Rig before?' Stevenoak asked.

'Who's Pike? Who's Rig? I never knew no Rig,' the old man replied. 'I know some of them by name but I never knew no Rig.'

Mex had been nosing around in the trees off to the left. He came back slowly. 'They had a camp out there,' he told Jordan. 'Tipis and tents and stuff. Been camping there for some time, looks like.'

The old man shrugged his scrawny shoulders. 'Any man or woman passing here wants to bide a while, I ain't discouraging him. It ain't nothing to me and I don't ask no questions.'

Jordan emptied the remains of the coffee on the ground and handed the mug to the old man. 'Thanks for the coffee and thanks for your hospitality.' He grinned. 'Guess we'll be rolling on.'

'Pleasure to welcome you.' The old man winked at Beth.

They mounted up and rode over to where the Quantrills had had their camp.

'The old man knows more than he says,' Stevenoak said.

The old man had started to play his mouth organ. Though he wasn't exactly an accomplished performer he could bring out quite a passable tune.

The camp among the trees was extensive. Round it the ground was churned up and you could see where the tipis had been pitched, most of them small. You could also see where the horses had been hitched. More to the point, you could see where the whole bunch of the Quantrills had struck camp and ridden away.

'What do you aim to do?' Stevenoak asked Jordan in a suspicious tone.

Jordan and Beth exchanged glances.

Jordan said, 'We ride on, find out where those Quantrills are now.'

Mex and Beth nodded. 'Nothing else we can do.'

Stevenoak looked decidedly uncomfortable. 'I can't do that,' he said. 'I got to ride back to Redsville. I have duties there. Like the old man said, my jurisdiction doesn't reach as far as this. If a man commits a crime in town I need to arrest him and inform the judge. That's my responsibility.'

'Even if a man brings a body into town on the back of a horse?' Beth said with irony.

'Yes, ma'am,' the lawman said. 'Especially then.' He glanced at Jordan. 'I guess your story about how Rig died seems to check out. Seems you also met that man Coulter out here last night. The note Mex found at the Holdern place supports that right enough.' He nodded and avoided Jordan's eye. 'But I need to tell you something, Mr Jordan. Far as I'm concerned you're still under arrest. You come back to Redsville, I have to put you in the lockup till the judge comes. I want you to understand that. And that's the law.

'When I come into town you can arrest me again,' Jordan said. 'Meantime, I've got pressing business to attend to.'

Stevenoak shrugged and turned his horse away from the deserted camping place. Then he turned in the saddle and spoke over his shoulder, 'Ain't much you can do against that Quantrill bunch. Could be twenty of them at least.'

'Maybe thirty,' Mex said.

Stevenoak turned his horse and rode away. The old man was still wheezing away at the mouth organ.

'Now what do we aim to do?' Beth asked Jordan.

The muscles on the side of Jordan's jaw tightened and then relaxed. 'I want for you to go back to your people, make sure everything's OK there.'

Beth was smiling grimly. He saw the flecks of gold darting in her eyes. 'You know I can't do that, Nat.'

Jordan gave Mex an appealing look that said, *What do you do with a stubborn woman like this?*

Mex nodded slightly and grinned and shrugged. This was a situation in which he couldn't get involved. So he sidled away, almost out of earshot.

Jordan tried again. He gripped Beth's hand and held it tight. 'Listen,' he said. 'What Mex and me are going to do might be dangerous – very dangerous. You heard what Stevenoak said and he's right. You have to know that. And I don't want you to be involved in bloodshed.' He shook his head, struggling for the right words. 'I want you safe, Beth. I need you safe.' He squeezed her gentle hand in his.

She looked right into his eyes and smiled. Then her jaw tightened. 'Nat,' she said quietly, 'I know what you have to do and I know it's dangerous, but I'm going along with you and I shan't be a burden to you. So get that through your head. There's nothing you can do to stop me, and *that's that.*' The last two words were spoken with such a strong emphasis that Jordan knew he had to surrender.

He squeezed Beth's hand again and released it.

Mex turned his horse, and together, the three of them rode. The way ahead would be difficult and dangerous . . . but maybe clearer than they expected.

Not much need for Mex's remarkable tracking skills. Those Quantrills had left a trail that a blind mule could follow. It led away over the prairie to a place that was thinly peppered with small homesteads and farms. Jordan was torn between returning to Redsville and getting a posse together and going on.

'Nobody in Redsville will believe us,' Beth said.

'We have to ride on and track those Quantrills down,' Mex agreed.

Deep in his bones Jordan knew they were right.

Before sundown they approached a farm that seemed quiet and peaceable. Jordan looked over the scene with the telescope an old sailor had given him and saw a skinny woman come out of the cabin to throw down feed for the hens. In a pen close by there were two or three quite well-groomed horses feeding from a bundle of hay. Nothing much more save for a fairly substantial barn and an area of vegetable garden behind it.

'Good place for a whole bunch of *hombres* to stay,' Mex remarked.

'I'm going down to take a looksee,' Jordan said. 'Shelter and feed for the horses . . . and maybe a little chow for us.'

He rode down to the homestead real easy. The woman looked up and, shading her eyes against the light, saw him She stretched her back with her hands on her hips and watched him judiciously. She had the granite face of a woman who had lived through rough times. But she didn't flinch or retreat into the cabin to grab a gun. She just waited, squinted up at him as he meandered down.

He touched the brim of his Stetson. 'Evening, ma'am,' he said amiably.

'You want something, stranger?' she asked in a cracked tone.

'Just looking for a likely place to stay and, maybe, a bite to eat,' he said. He patted his saddle-bag. 'We can pay our way, of course.'

'Travellers?' a voice said from somewhere close. Jordan turned his head to see a man in the doorway with a shotgun trained on him. 'We don't welcome no strangers here abouts. Too many thieves and desperadoes in these parts.'

Jordan nodded. 'I seen a few myself.'

The man came forward with the shotgun on Jordan. 'You a military man?' he asked with his eyes narrowed. 'You sound like a military man, look like a military man.'

Jordan saw he was tall – maybe six one or two – and had been well muscled though he had let himself turn to flab. There was something mean and untrusting in his piggy eyes that Jordan didn't care for.

'I've done soldiering,' Jordan said. 'I put that behind me after the war.'

'War's been over ten years,' the man said. 'Pretty bad deal too.'

Jordan didn't pursue the matter.

The man gestured with the shotgun. 'You alone?'

'Not exactly,' Jordan admitted. 'Just rode down to get the lie of the land. Like you said there's a lot of bad company around. I've got a woman – a lady, I should say – and a Mexican man with me.'

The big man darted a look at the stand of trees above. 'Up there, are they, keeping me covered in case of trouble?'

Jordan grinned. 'You could say that. A waddy doesn't look for trouble but he has to face it when it comes.'

The man gave a low chuckle. 'That's my way of thinking.'

He paused to consider matters. 'Did I hear you to tell my woman something about payment?' he asked.

Jordan nodded. 'We can pay a fair price for what we get.'

The shotgun seemed to waver a little. The man gave a brief nod. 'You can bring your partners in. My woman will give you what you need in the way of victuals. You have a mind to it you can sleep in the barn. Plenty of room and plenty of straw. A few beasts but they shouldn't disturb your beauty sleep.'

Jordan looked into the barn. Like the man said, at one end there were brood mares and a mule. The other end was corralled off and there was a ladder leading to a hayloft.

'You can sleep up there if you've mind to it,' the man said brusquely. 'You can eat in the house. My woman knows how to cook good. I think we got chicken stew and maybe a few dumplings in line for tonight. Don't eat much myself.'

Jordan searched the barn with his eyes. No sign of other inhabitants other than rats and feral cats. He went out into the yard and gave a brief signal to Beth and Mex and they came riding down the hill.

The man looked them over with shrewd suspicious eyes. He was still holding his shotgun at the trail. 'Mexican, ain't you?' he said. 'You been up this way long?'

'Long enough,' Mex said briefly.

They released the horses in the corral and went into the barn. The man was at the door, watching them with his shotgun trailing. The woman had come into the barn. Her eyes softened a little when she saw Beth.

'You come from far off?' she asked in her cracked voice

'Other side of Redsville,' Beth said.

'Been a deal of trouble down that way,' the man remarked from the door. 'They say there was a hold-up on the railroad to Kansas City from the east a little while back. Did you hear about that?'

119

Jordan dropped his saddle on the hay. 'Heard about it,' he said.

'They say a man died in the caboose,' the man continued.

'That's the truth,' Jordan replied.

'They lynched a man in his own home down there,' the woman said. 'Least that's what we heard.'

'I believe that's so,' Jordan replied.

'You can come along into the house when you're set,' the man said. 'My woman will dish out your stew.'

The woman ducked her head and went into the house.

'Tell you something,' Mex said when they had unloaded their stuff and made themselves as comfortable as possible in the barn.

'I know what you're going to say,' Jordan relied. 'There's something ornery about those two, 'specially the man.'

'Goldarned suspicious,' Mex said. 'I figure they know why we're here.'

Jordan straightened up.

Beth was looking uneasily at Mex. 'I had that feeling too,' she said.

'That's why they tried to draw us out on the train robbery and my pa's hanging. That what you mean?'

Mex looked at him squarely and said nothing for a moment. 'Those Quantrills have been here,' he said at last.

'You mean right here in this barn?' Jordan said.

Mex nodded.

'How can you know that?'

Mex raised his head like a dog that catches a scent. He spoke in a measured tone. 'I know it like a hound knows a rat has been around. That's how I know it.'

They were silent for a second or two. Nobody contradicted Mex; when Mex said a thing he always hit the nail square.

They went into the house. The woman was at the stove, cooking up the chicken stew. The man was at the table sitting behind a bottle of whiskey. Jordan saw by the expression on his face that he had already drunk more than one glass.

'Set you down,' the man greeted somewhat more jovially than he had when he greeted them. 'I took my victuals earlier. My main sustenance comes from this here.' He held up the bottle and shook it.

The woman gave a grunt and dished dollops of stew onto wooden platters and left the three strangers to eat. The man was onto his third glass of whiskey and he started to sing in a hard unmelodious tone like something was gnawing at his insides. The woman looked at him uneasily but said nothing.

The stew was quite appetizing and the three visitors attacked it with relish.

'My woman cooks good,' the man said, winking at Beth. 'Are you a good cooking woman or do you decorate the house like a wall flower or something?'

'I can cook,' Beth said. She glanced at the woman who gave her a brief nod as if to say: *don't rise to the bait.*

The man looked at Jordan and then at Mex. 'You got a fine, good-looking woman here,' he announced in a jeering tone. 'You taking a honeymoon trip together or something?'

The muscles at the side of Jordan's jaw tensed but he said nothing.

The woman bustled around. 'Have another plate of stew?'

'We got plenty,' the man interjected. 'Just as long as you can pay, it's a deal.'

121

*

They went back into the barn and spread their bedrolls. Jordan and Mex drifted off immediately but Beth felt restless. She checked the horses and later came back into the barn and shook Jordan. A soldier sleeps deeply but wakes easily, and Jordan came back from his dreams immediately.

Beth put her head close to his and whispered, 'There's been a bust up!'

Jordan was on his feet at once, buckling on his gunbelt. Before he reached the door of the barn, Mex was on his feet with a gun in his hand.

'That man's been shouting and beating up on the woman. You can hear them now.'

They went out under the stars and listened. It didn't take long. The man inside the cabin was raving drunk. Jordan could hear him shouting and stamping around. The woman screamed and, from the sound, was hurled against the wall.

'Oh, that poor woman!' Beth said. 'That man is set to kill her!'

Before they could make a move, there was a muffled shot from inside the cabin, the door was thrown open, and the man came lumbering out with a pistol in his hand. 'Where are those spies!' he shouted, in a voice blurred by booze.

He came staggering into the yard and fired a couple more shots into the sky. The horses in the corral whinnied and spooked.

'What the hell!' the man shouted. 'This is my place! This is my spread! I do as I please around here!'

He turned back towards the house and focused on the three figures standing close by the doorway.

'What?' he roared. 'You spying again? I know what you're doing. You spying out on the Quantrill bunch! I know you! I smell you a mile off.'

He staggered towards Jordan with his gun in his hand. Jordan moved with the speed of a mountain lion. The gun spun away out of the man's hand. Jordan's left fist connected with his chest and his right fist jabbed at his jaw. The man's head snapped back and he sprawled with his arms out in the yard.

Jordan nursed his bare knuckles, and the woman appeared in the doorway. 'What have you done?' she gasped.

'Saved a deal of fuss,' Jordan said.

The woman came out and looked at her partner lying face up on the ground. 'You've killed him,' she said in amazement.

'He's just out cold,' Jordan reassured her. 'He'll wake with a head like the deep rings of hell, but *he will wake.*'

They gathered together the unconscious man and hauled him into the house and dumped him down on a cot. That man was no lightweight.

The woman was shaking like a ghost had got into her marrow. Beth put her arms round her and made soothing noises. The woman grabbed at a chair and sat down with her head on the table and sobbed. Jordan saw she had a blueish bruise coming up on the side of her cheek.

'What do I do?' the woman wailed. She raised her head and appealed to Beth. 'What do I do?'

Beth shook her head and stroked the woman's brow. It was hard to see such a toughened stick of a woman so broken up.

Presently she calmed down a little and raised her head again. 'He ain't usually like this; it's when he hits the bottle he gets ornery. When he wakes up, he'll be sorry. It's just the booze gets to him. There's been a lot of stressful things lately.'

'What stressful things, ma'am?' Jordan asked her.

The woman threw a look of panic at the door behind which the man was sleeping. 'Things like those raiders. . . .' Her voice trailed off and she tried to hold back her words with her clenched fist.

'You mean those Quantrills?' Mex prompted.

A look of fear darted across her face. Then she seemed to struggle to master her terror. 'Yes,' she said. 'The Quantrills, the man who calls himself Quantrill the Second.'

'Coulter,' Jordan prompted.

'Yes. Sometimes they call him Captain Coulter,' she said. 'You know him, don't you?'

Jordan nodded. 'Served with him in the war.' He explained how he had been on the train the so-called Quantrills had held up and how the raiders had lynched his father.

The woman stared at him in amazement. 'That's terrible! That's what Ed figured. Thought you were set on bringing us trouble. That's what set him drinking like that.'

'We don't bring trouble, ma'am,' Jordan assured her. 'Trouble comes looking for us.' He leaned forward across the table. 'Those men who call themselves Quantrill Raiders, they've been here, haven't they?'

'They been in your barn,' Mex suggested.

The woman made as if to speak and then drew back. Then she made up her mind to speak. 'They've been here,' she admitted. 'And you're right, they were in the barn. They had a meeting there. That man Coulter spoke like he was talking to some sort of political rally. All loud and thunder stuff. They were going to start a new war, bring back the old way and undo the wrongs the North had inflicted on the South.' She paused to point a wavering finger towards the door. 'I was out there listening. I heard it all.'

'Where was Ed?' Beth asked.

She paused to gulp in another breath. 'He was right

there in that barn listening and cheering. They were all cheering and drinking booze and stamping like madmen. That man Coulter is mad as a coot. You know that? He's got the wrath of Satan in him!' She stared around, wide eyed. She looked at the door again. 'You mustn't blame Ed,' she said suddenly. 'He don't mean nothing. He just got carried away like the rest. Ed's no fighting man. He just wants to be left in peace.'

'He beat up on you though, didn't he?' Both said.

The woman grimaced. 'He don't mean nothing. That's the drink roaring through his body. It's like being possessed. When he comes to, he'll just be sick and quiet as a lamb.'

Jordan nodded grimly. 'Ed's a follower, ma'am,' he said. 'Those Quantrills wouldn't have come here without Ed's say-so, would they?'

The woman tried to speak again but stopped to get her breath. 'He's just a weak man,' she said. 'He does things afore he thinks. He just fell in with some of those Quantrills in a saloon he goes to up north. They turned his mind. But you won't do no harm on him, will you?'

Jordan shrugged. 'Ed stays sleeping we leave him be. He comes out roaring and threatening again, that's another story.'

'You won't kill him, will you?' she pleaded.

Jordan looked at her straight. 'We don't aim to kill anyone, ma'am,' he said. 'But sometimes you have to kill. That's a thing we can't avoid.'

Again she was struggling, making up her mind to speak. 'You promise me you won't harm Ed, I'll tell you something . . . something you need to know.'

The three visitors fixed their eyes on the woman and waited. It was a minute or two before she could make up her mind to speak.

125

'I heared something in the barn that night,' she half whispered. 'It's what those raiders aim to do next.'

Jordan nodded and stared at her intently. Beth took the woman's arm and patted her hand to reassure her.

The woman's voice sank to below a whisper. 'Those raiders said the next thing they do is ride on Redsville, burn the town down, show the country all round how they mean to revive the cause of the South.'

Beth gave a sharp intake of breath.

Jordan was still looking intently at the woman. 'When do they mean to do this, ma'am?' he asked.

She hesitated a moment. 'Could be tomorrow,' she said. 'Tomorrow around sundown. That's what they said.' She glanced towards the door again. 'But one thing I can promise you, my man Ed won't be there.'

CHAPTER TEN

Jordan shelled out for the horse care and the food they'd eaten and they rode away from the homestead to a likely place to sleep for the night. Nobody wanted to spend more time in that barn with a crazy man on the loose.

They chose a sheltered spot close to a fast-flowing stream where they could replenish their canteens and wash up. When they had set camp and hobbled the horses, they lit a fire and sat around to discuss their next move.

'No choice,' Mex said. 'We need to get back to Redsville soon as we can.'

Beth agreed. 'That woman was talking the truth.'

Jordan agreed. He had seen already they had no alternative.

As soon as the first glimmer of light showed in the East, they were in the saddle headed for Redsville.

They rode into town around midday and went straight for the sheriff's office. Sheriff Stevenoak was sitting in his chair with his thumbs tucked into his suspenders talking to one of his deputies. When the three figures loomed in the doorway, his mouth fell open and he reached for his hat.

'Didn't expect to see you so soon,' he said.

'Didn't expect to be back in town,' Jordan told him.

'You come to hand yourself in?' Stevenoak said.

'We've come to wise you up on what we heard,' Jordan replied.

Stevenoak dithered as usual, didn't know what to say to keep up his position with the deputy who was eyeing Jordan and the other three with awe. Name of Jefferson, Jordan remembered. Usually worked around the general store unless the sheriff called on his services. Could be a blabber-mouth and none too bright like the sheriff.

'You want to make some kind of testimony for the judge you got to wait in the cells. That's the law,' Stevenoak said.

'I don't think I can do that,' Jordan said. 'Got things to do. Can't do them in that draughty lock-up of yours.'

Stevenoak's eyes roamed to Jordan's gunbelt. He glanced towards Mex who didn't look encouraging. So he switched to Beth.

'You still rousting around, Miss Beth?' he joked feebly. ' 'Bout time you went back to your family. They must be missing you real bad. Probably wondering where you went.'

'They'll find out soon enough,' Beth said. 'We need to talk to you in private, Mr Stevenoak.'

Stevenoak looked about like he was searching for a snake hiding under his desk.

'You want for me to go, Miss Armitage?' Jefferson said.

Stevenoak nodded. 'Go across to the Washington, have a drink on me. I'll join you later,' he said.

Jefferson made a quick retreat. He had been one of Stevenoak's original posse when they came to the Armitage place to commiserate over old man Jordan's lynching.

The sheriff spread his hands. 'Why don't we set down and talk a little. I can see you've come to discuss the Qauntrill bunch and I'm good and ready to listen.'

There was a chair and a bench in the office. Beth and Mex took the bench and Jordan occupied the chair.

'Fire away,' the sheriff said.

Jordan told him everything that had happened after he left them at the old man's shack. He gave a straight account with no frills as Beth and Mex sat still as statues listening.

When Jordan had finished his account, the sheriff leaned back in his chair with his thumbs hooked into his suspenders. 'What you're telling me is a man got drunk and thrashed around a bit and then his wife told you those Quantrills held a meeting in the barn and decided to ride in on Redsville and set fire to the place at sundown today? Is that what you're telling me?' His eyes were filled with a kind of dancing scepticism.

Jordan nodded. 'That's what the lady said.'

Beth spoke out: 'And I believe her, the way she said it.'

Stevenoak started tapping his desk with a pencil. 'So that's what she told you and you believed her, Miss Beth.' He leaned back with a jeering look in his eyes. 'You know what I think: someone tells me I'm gonna find a ten-dollar bill on the sidewalk when I step across Main Street, eh? Is that the way it is?' He nodded in a fatherly way. 'Miss Beth, I have great respect for you; I know you to be a very truth-ful lady. But do you expect me to believe what you're telling me?'

'It's the truth, Mr Stevenoak!' Beth's eyes flashed.

Mex stirred. 'You can't afford not to believe it, Mr Stevenoak,' he growled.

Then Jordan spoke again. 'Those so-called Quantrills held up a train coming in to Kansas City. Then they killed my pa for speaking out here in Redsville in favour of the Union cause. Now they aim to make a big gesture by attack-ing the town. Those raiders are as mean as a bunch of rattlesnakes and that's the way we have to treat them!'

Stevenoak stared at Jordan and he looked real thought-ful for a while. 'Suppose I take this seriously – and I don't figure I am – what d'you expect me to do?'

Jordan nodded. 'First off, you could send a wire through to Kansas City. The military need to know about this.'

The glimmer of ridicule appeared in Stevenoak's eyes. 'You want me to call in the army on the strength of a crazy woman's rumour?' He rolled his eyes round the office in astonishment.

'The second thing you do,' Jordan said intently, 'is to gather the people of Redsville together so, when the raiders come, we're as ready as we can be. Even if the military in Kansas City take your message seriously they wouldn't get here in time to stop the Quantrills anyway. So whatever happens, we're on our own here.'

Stevenoak looked astonished. 'You trying to make me look a fool in front of the community, Mr Jordan?'

Jordan shook his head. Instead of saying *you always look a fool, Mr Stevenoak*, he said, 'You do nothing, there could be a deal of blood on your hands. Those Quantrills are dead set on starting a new war.'

That made Stevenoak think. The look of ridicule faded from his lips and his brow creased in a frown.

Beth was studying him closely. She knew how stubborn he could be and what a slug-like brain he had. But he was the man with the badge of authority.

'Nat's right,' she said. 'You can't afford to sit on your hands and do nothing. You have to act, Sheriff.'

Stevenoak still wasn't sure. He shook his head. 'You hold up a locomotive, that's one thing. Attacking a whole town is something else again. I'm gonna go over to the Washington and chew on a doughnut. Help me make up my mind on this.'

He had made no further mention of locking Jordan up in the hoosegow. So Jordan, Beth and Mex walked onto Main Street to figure out tactics. Jordan noticed the curtains of McGill's office were drawn tight which meant he was either taking a nap or had pulled out like he had said.

'You looking for that Pinkerton man?' A familiar voice came from behind them.

Jordan turned to see Preacher Man. He was wearing his usual outfit: bowler at an angle, whiskers trailing over his cheeks, tweed vest and jacket, and he was carrying his fiddle case and a carpet-bag in his left hand. 'I've done my best for the nation,' he proclaimed. 'I aim to go back to Kansas City and figure what to do next. There's only so much juice in a small town like this. I wouldn't want to suck it dry.' He gave a friendly chuckle. 'By the way, that Pinkerton man, McGill, pulled out yesterday after he visited with you in the hoosegow. He was real sore about you killing Pike.' Preacher Man wrinkled his nose. 'Being a detective McGill doesn't care to be deceived none. That killing rattled him up real good. Probably going to Kansas City to lick his wounds.'

'So you're headed back to the city yourself?' Jordan shook his head.

Preacher Man seemed to waver. He glanced up and down Main Street. 'Had a mind to, like I said. 'Cept I just heard a word passing between Sheriff Stevenoak and that deputy – name's Jefferson, I believe. So I think I might change my mind and stay after all.'

'Could be better for a thinking fiddler like you to leave,' Jordan advised. 'Might be a deal of trouble before the next stage leaves for Kansas City.'

Preacher Man sniffed the air. 'As you know, I don't use the stage and don't know much about trouble,' he said, 'except what I've seen. But I listen good and put two and two together like the Good Book says.'

Jordan couldn't figure where that came in the Good Book but he didn't enquire further.

Preacher Man stepped in closer. 'I heard rumours on the

wind, you know,' he said.

'What did the wind say?'

Preacher Man raised his eyebrows. 'The wind said a deal about you and those Quantrills. Some folk think you're still working for that bunch. There's a lot of uneasiness and bad mouthing in this town right now.'

Jordan nodded. 'So, what's your opinion, my friend?'

Preacher Man held his head on one side and screwed his lips up in a grin. 'As I said, I only know what I see, and I see plenty. That man Coulter is bad medicine. I knew that when he held up the train. He's the kind of fanatic who won't let a thing stand in his path when he makes up his mind what to do.'

Jordan hesitated and then decided to speak. 'I'll tell you this, partner,' he said. 'Captain Coulter aims to lead those so-called Quantrills into town this night. They mean to wreck and burn. That's what I hear.'

'This very night,' Preacher Man muttered to himself. 'You mean at sundown this day?'

'That's what I mean,' Jordan said. 'It's all hearsay, but it could be true.'

Preacher Man put his carpet-bag and his violin case down on the street. He removed his bowler, studied it for a moment, and then put it on his head again. 'In that case I shall stick around here in Redsville.' He looked at Mex and then at Beth. 'That's what I'm gonna do; stay here and help you out whatever you decide to do.'

They went into the Washington and saw Stevenoak and his side kick Jefferson huddled in a corner drinking something that looked like whiskey. Stevenoak needs something strong to sustain him, Jordan thought. What McGill said about him was right: he hasn't got the balls to do a damned thing at a time like this.

132

They sat behind a table as far away from the sheriff as possible. The barman, Lem, came over looking like a friendly bear. He and Preacher Man had worked up a good relationship and Lem had even been seen to dance to his fiddle playing in the evening. They ordered beefsteak and all the side orders, washed down with beer.

When the plates were on the table Preacher Man said, 'This meal's on me. We have to work together, we need to eat together. Like the three musketeers.' He turned to Lem, the friendly bear. 'Decided to stay on another night and cheek out tomorrow if I'm still alive if that's OK?'

The barman laughed and they proceeded with their meal. Jordan noticed that the sheriff and his deputy Jefferson had slid out quietly. Maybe Stevenoak intended to gather together a few citizens to make a stand. Maybe he intended to go home to his wife, or take a nap in the office. Either way it didn't signify.

When they had eaten their meal, they slipped out of the bar by a back door. The barman probably thought they were going up to Preacher Man's room to deal a round of poker. In fact, Preacher Man dumped his carpet-bag on the bed and laid his fiddle reverently beside it. 'Bide there, my beauty,' he said. 'You sleep while the rest of us work for the good of the community.'

They continued up several flights of stairs to a door that opened onto a flat roof. The Washington was the tallest building in town. It reached to three floors and it had a fancy façade with a curlicue scroll under which in fancy lettering it boasted *The Washington Hotel* picked out in letters of gold, red and green.

Jordan and Mex went forward to peer over the edge of the roof, a perfect place to kneel and look down over Main Street. It was a long way down. From there you could see horses and people moving around like toys.

Jordan stood up and studied the horizon all round with his telescope. It was the best place to look out over the town and the rolling prairie beyond.

Beth and Preacher Man were over by the door. Both were uneasy about heights but they braced themselves to edge forward and look out over the parapet. The façade gave them an illusion of safety.

'We need Winchesters and ammunition,' Jordan said. 'Plenty shells.' He laid his Winchester on the roof close behind the parapet. Mex laid his Winchester beside it.

'I don't have any kind of gun,' Preacher Man apologized. 'Swore I'd never use one, but I could if I needed to.'

Beth hadn't got a gun either, not even a derringer which wouldn't have been any use anyway up there on the roof.

Jordan and Mex exchanged glances.

Mex nodded. 'I bring guns. You wait.' He disappeared through the door to the roof.

It seemed a long time before he reappeared but he kept his word. He brought three Winchester '66s and his pockets were stuffed with cartridges, enough for a good-sized battle. Nobody asked where they had come from, or how he had managed to sneak them away without being seen. They laid the weapons down on the roof and waited. Two men used to toting guns, one woman of real grit, and a fiddler who had never fired a shot in anger, against how many – was it twenty or thirty, hardened fanatics? If those Quantrills came!

It seemed a long time before the sun turned to a ball of gold and started to sink down behind the buildings. Maybe this is all a bunch of damned nonsense, Jordan thought. Maybe that hard-faced woman with the crazy husband painted a picture to lead us like steers down a dry gulch with no way out!

If those raiders were really set on burning down the

town, would they come roaring and hooting, shooting off their guns every whichway? And, if they did, how many could he and Mex kill before they overwhelmed the place?

He turned to Beth lying close beside him on the roof. She stretched out her hand as if to say, *be brave; we're together; we can get through this.*

Mex had moved away further down the roof. Preacher Man was hugging his Winchester like he didn't know which end the bullet might come out!

Jordan's mind went round in a circle and came back again. This is all a big play; I think they call it a farce, he thought. But, as he was sliding into doubt and despondency again, something happened and it wasn't quite what he expected. There was a movement at the end of Main Street towards the west where the sun's last rays were dying. There was no roaring and no fury. Just a band of men riding. He could hear them, but he couldn't see them. But he saw and heard Redsville's response: doors banged shut, lamps were extinguished, there were cries of terror. The people of Redsville knew that something ugly was about to happen.

Mex moved back along the roof. 'They're on their way,' he said, and for some reason, he sounded excited like he was anticipating a great feast.

'How many?' Beth asked.

'Maybe twenty and they're carrying torches,' Mex said.

Now Jordan could see the flaming torches advancing down Main Street. They looked kind of lively and cheerful as they advanced, jogging along towards the Washington. But there was something purposeful and relentless about them too. This is no rabble: this is an army, Jordan thought.

Preacher Man rose with his weapon and peered over the parapet. 'These men are like soldiers,' he gasped.

Then came another movement. They turned their heads to see a second small army approaching from the other end of Main Street. The claws, one at each end of the street, were converging to crush the town!

'Dear Gawd!' Preacher Man said. 'What have we got into? We can't fight an army like this!'

Then they noticed another thing. These slowly advancing men were wearing masks. Their faces and shoulders were draped in white with holes cut out for their eyes. They were carrying a flag, the flag of the old Confederate Army.

'Like ghosts!' Preacher Man whispered. 'Like spectres riding in from the past.'

Now the townspeople were peering out through their windows, opening their doors a crack to watch the passing spectacle.

'What can we hope to do?' Beth said breathlessly.

Jordan was searching intently among the men below. Coulter must be there somewhere, leading his command. Something seemed to grab at Jordan's throat. This was Coulter's army. These men tramping the dust were Coulter's men. In the recent war, he, Jordan, would have been part of that army.

Young as the youngest who donned the gray.
True as the truest who wore it,
Brave as the bravest he marched away. . . .

The words sprang spontaneously into his mind.

But the thread soon broke. An alien figure rode among the white masked figures. His head was bare and his arms were tied behind his back.

'That's McGill, the Pinkerton man!' Preacher Man gasped. 'Looks like they're holding him prisoner!'

Jordan peered down at the advancing men. He would have recognized McGill from his clothes and his portly figure, but now he wasn't smoking one of those Havana cigars. In fact, even from high up on the the roof of the Washington, without looking through his telescope, Jordan saw that McGill was shaking with terror.

He soon saw the reason. One of the riders rode forward and snake a noose over McGill's neck. Someone threw the rope over a hook above the sidewalk, and one of the riders started to speak in a loud voice like he was making a proclamation. As soon as the man spoke, Jordan knew he was listening to Coulter.

Coulter raised his voice and shouted, 'This man is a betrayer. He has betrayed the cause. We caught him running for cover like a scared deer and now we decree he must be punished like the traitor he is.'

A chorus of cheers went up from the masked men and there was a muffled groan from the watching townsfolk.

'Let this be a lesson to all traitors!' Coulter shouted. 'If you're with us, you live! If you betray us, you die!'

As he spoke, McGill was struggling feverishly to free his hands. He had opened his mouth to scream when Coulter's hand came down and a man whipped up McGill's horse. McGill swung out at the end of the rope in a wide circle like a sackful of hay. Yet instead of dropping like a stone, he struck out with his legs and hit a post. The post broke his fall so that he swung in a pendulum, jerking and kicking to save himself. His neck wasn't broken and he would be a long agonized time dying.

'My God, poor man!' Beth covered her face with her hands and looked away.

Preacher Man groaned and started to retch behind the fancy façade.

The muscles at the side of Jordan's tensed and he chewed hard. He steadied himself against the sign, raised his Winchester, caught his breath, and fired a single shot.

McGill was still lashing out with his legs, struggling to

gasp the air when the bullet struck him. He jerked, kicked out in one final spasm, and hung limp.

'My Gawd, you killed him!' Preacher Man gasped.

'Act of mercy,' Mex muttered between his teeth.

'This is the day!' Jordan said. He leaned over the parapet and started to fire on men in the white masks. He was looking for Coulter but Coulter had ridden close under the ramada. They could hear him shouting orders but Jordan couldn't get a bead on him. Now the dark raiders in the white masks did what they had meant to do. They started hurling their flaming torches through windows and doors. People were screaming. Riders had fallen, horses had reared but Jordan knew he and Mex and Beth couldn't hope to win against this horde. Some of the gunmen below had already located them and were pumping off shots in their direction, and the façade bucked like it had become a wild horse. A hole was suddenly punched through an inch from Mex's head. Another took off Preacher Man's bowler but nobody stopped to notice he was bald. Even Beth was busy pumping shot in the direction of the wild men below.

Then the thing Jordan expected and feared happened. Flames came belching out from the sides of the Washington. The whole place stared to rumble and roar. Screams of terror and pain rose from below.

'We're in a fire trap!' Beth exclaimed.

Jordan knew she was right. He and Mex were still firing shots at the riders below. The horses were rearing; the riders were shooting wildly into the hotel and in through townsfolk's doors. He saw one more rider throw up his arms and fall before he acted.

'We got to move. We're gonna fry!' he said to Beth as he drew back from the edge of the roof and looked for an escape route.

'Over the rooftops!' Mex said.

Preacher Man turned frantically. 'My violin!' he shouted. 'I can't go without my violin!'

'You can't go in there!' Beth cried, grabbing his vest.

Preacher Man shook his head, tore himself away, flung open the door, and disappeared into the hotel.

He'll burn, Jordan thought. We don't get out of here pronto, we'll all burn. He grabbed Beth's arm and together they ran, crouching, to the end of the roof. Clouds of black smoke were billowing up with tongues of scorching fire. It seemed like the gaping edge of hell.

'We gotta jump!' Mex said. 'We got get across there!' But it was a long way and another floor down. A man would need wings to get across and, anyway, Beth was too short and too small to leap that gap.

Mex was searching along the roof. 'This way!' he shouted. 'There's a walkway here!'

There was an iron ladder set into the wall, leading below. Did it go right down, or did it end in a cloud of black smoke? How could they know?

Mex was already on the ladder working his way down. Jordan lowered himself on to the stairway which seemed none too secure. 'Step onto the ladder and we'll go down together,' he said to Beth.

Beth didn't hesitate. She wasn't a woman to scream or back away. She climbed down onto the iron stairway between Jordan's arms and together they edged down into the darkness.

They had to be quick before the black billowing smoke overcame them. Otherwise they would drop like fried insects into the darkness!

'It ends here!' Mex said from below. Jordan looked down and saw the iron stairway dangling in space where it had broken off. But there was another more secure stairway with a handrail on the opposite building. Mex was reaching out for it but he couldn't quite make it, couldn't get enough purchase to leap across.

'Hold on tight, baby!' Jordan said to Beth.

He pushed his foot against the wall and reached for the other stairway. Not quite. Try again. He pushed with his foot and the stairway they were on began to creak. Then his fingers made contact with the other stairway. It was firm and he got a grip. On his right he was on the swinging ladder; on his left was the secure one. 'Get across, Beth,' he said. 'Use my body and get across.'

Beth edged down and made a grab for his arm. She breathed in quickly and reached out for the other stairway. The ladder they had been on swung out from the wall. Mex was pushing at the wall with his foot and she got across.

Jordan swung over to join her. Mex was suspended like a spider on the end of the breaking ladder. Jordan leaned out to steady the iron rail. 'Come up and get across!' Jordan said to Mex.

Mex was already moving up steadily. Any second the rusting framework would break off and send him into the darkness below. He grabbed at Jordan's ankle and heaved himself across. The old ladder creaked and swung against the wall with one side of it severed.

They climbed onto the roof of the neighbouring building as the hotel exploded in a ball of fire.

CHAPTER ELEVEN

No time to hang around. No time to rest, The scorching flames sprang out from the Washington and they ran to find a door and a passage. They dragged open the door and hurtled down a long corridor and downstairs past screaming women and children to the lower floor.

'Get out! Get out!' Beth said to the screaming women.

Mex was ahead, searching for an exit. He found a door back of the building and burst out into air thick with smoke. Jordan stayed back with Beth to make sure she got out safely. They ran coughing and choking away from the building.

'Damned right!' Mex gasped. 'Those devil raiders mean to burn down the whole town.'

'Nothing we can do,' Jordan said. 'We gotta keep going.'

They moved down the back of the buildings and rested against a wall to recover. They could still hear the roar of the flames and smell the acrid, choking smoke but behind it there was the crackle of gunfire, intense and fierce. There seemed to be a battle raging with firing from two sides. Could it be the citizens of Redsville were hitting back against their attackers? It hardly seemed possible that Redsville could have mustered so many arms and so much determination.

As they recovered their breath in the walkway between two buildings, a man in a white mask came running towards them. He held a Colt in his right hand and he looked ready to shoot down anyone who got in his way. As he encountered Jordan he fired a wild shot and it came close. Jordan felt the hot blast of the bullet as it winged by his ear. As the masked figure blundered on towards him, Jordan caught at its arm and wrenched it back against the wall. He jabbed the masked man in the stomach, once, twice, and then gripped his throat and slammed him against the wall. The masked figure crumpled and slid down onto the ground. Jordan stooped and took up the Colt. It might be useful. They'd had to abandon all those Winchesters Mex had mustered on the roof of the Washington.

'Strange thing,' Mex said close to his ear. 'There's a gunfight going on. What in damnation's happening here?'

'What's happening is we're not the only ones getting in the way of those raiders. Seems like they've got big opposition,' Jordan said.

He went to the end of the walkway and had a quick look-see. The raiders were in a battle. They were shooting from left to right in the direction of the Washington and they were edging back. It wasn't a rout but an orderly retreat.

'What do we do now?' Beth asked breathlessly.

'We sit tight and wait,' Jordan said.

So they crouched down in the alley and watched.

The raiders were retreating, but they were far from finished. As they fell back they were still firing with some accuracy at the advancing men . . . whoever they were.

Presently the surge of battle passed on down Main Street to the end of town, and there was a lull. Two shadows fell across the end of the alleyway which shaped into men against the yellow dark background. They were dressed in army uniform and they had nervous guns trained on Jordan, Beth and Mex.

'You come out from behind there,' one of the soldiers shouted. 'Come out with your hands held high.'

They got their feet and held up their hands.

'Step out onto Main Street,' one of the soldiers ordered. He was trigger-nervous and battle tense. So they stepped out real slowly with their hands up.

An older man came forward through the smoke and he had the stripes of a sergeant on his sleeve. 'You been involved in this battle?' he demanded, looking down at the Colt in Jordan's hand.

Jordan remembered his escapes from the Union forces with Coulter in the war and it gave him a weird feeling like he should still be fighting now at Coulter's side. 'Been gunning against Coulter on the roof of the Washington.' he said. 'Got ourselves slightly singed from the fire.'

The sergeant held his head on one side and laughed. It was a sceptical unpleasant laugh. 'You know Coulter?' he demanded.

Jordan decided to tell the truth. 'Fought alongside him in the war. He was Captain Coulter in those days.'

The sergeant peered closely into Jordan's face like he was trying to read a coded message. 'You fought alongside Coulter on the rebel side?' he repeated.

Jordan shrugged. 'That's the way it was. But I got the pardon after the war. Fought at Bull Run and other places Coulter and I escaped together once or twice.'

'Well, now,' the sergeant nodded his head and grinned. 'I guess you'll be right glad to know we got Coulter and the rest of the rebel bunch pinned down just a short step down the street from here. We're waiting for them to put out the white flag and give themselves up.'

'Coulter won't like that,' Jordan said.

The sergeant gave a wry grin. 'Coulter don't have no choice in the matter. He either comes out or we smoke him out.'

'That wouldn't be the first time,' Jordan said. 'He must be getting used to the feeling.'

'Good thing we got here in time,' the sergeant reflected.

'How d'you come to be here anyway?' Jordan asked.

The sergeant shrugged. 'Got a wire through from one of our agents. Name of McGill. Seems he was right, too. Before he could ride back to Kansas City, they bushwhacked him and strung him up just opposite the Washington hotel. They tell me someone shot him as he hung there.'

'That was an act of mercy,' Mex said.

The sergeant looked at him with contempt. 'Where d'you come into this, cowboy?'

'I was there on the roof when they lynched McGill,' Mex said. 'We had information those Quantrills meant to burn the town down. We aimed to stop them.'

The sergeant chuckled. 'Nearly got yourself burned to a frazzle by the look of things.' His eye roamed over Beth. 'You in this too, ma'am? You should be at home looking after the kids. You know that?'

The other soldiers hooted with laughter. 'This is Beth Armitage,' Jordan said. 'She was up there with us on the roof. She fought too. She deserves some respect from you, Sergeant.'

'OK,' the sergeant said with a degree of apology. 'OK, ma'am, no offence intended.'

A soldier emerged from the gloom. 'Sergeant Winter, sir,' he said. 'Captain Taylor requests you come forward. They got those Rebs pinned down in a house at the end of Main Street. They left a litter of dead but some of them are

144

still holding out down there.'

The sergeant looked at Jordan again. 'You say you fought with Coulter; maybe you should come along with me. If Coulter's still alive in there, he might be glad to hear a friendly voice.'

'Got them on the run, you say?' another familiar voice piped up. It was Stevenoak. He came puffing up to the group cradling a Winchester in his arms like a determined soldier. 'Those damned rebels broke into my office, found the key to the gun store and took out half the Winchesters,' he complained. 'Lucky for them I wasn't around at the time.'

'Well, it didn't do them a whole of lot of good,' said the sergeant wryly. 'We killed half of them and the few that are left are pinned down in a building at the end of Main Street. We aim to smoke them out right now. You can come along if you've got a mind to it, Sheriff, not that Coulter and those Quantrills are going to take much account of the law around here.'

Stevenoak nodded and avoided making eye contact with Jordan.

The soldiers surged on down Main Street to where the Quantrills were said to be holed up.

Jordan made to follow, but stopped to hold on to Beth who was beside him, ready to go as well.

'Listen, baby,' he said. 'I don't think you need to be involved in this. Why don't you go back and see what needs to be done back there? There's women and children need attention and you could help in that.'

They could hear shouting close to the Washington where the town's firemen were struggling to put out the fire. Women and children and even men were staggering about in a hell of smoke and flame, stunned and bewildered by what was happening.

Beth stared through the murk for a moment and then made up her mind. 'I'll go,' she said, 'just as long as you promise me you won't take any risks. That Coulter is going to wish he killed you by that old man's shack out in the woods. You mustn't give him another chance.'

Jordan felt a dryness in his throat that he figured had nothing to do with the smoky air.

Beth turned and gave a brief wave before disappearing into the gloom. Mex grunted his approval.

Jordan and Mex moved on through a scene of mayhem. Masked figures and dead horses lay strewn along Main Street, and there were dead soldiers too. A wounded soldier came staggering past supported by two comrades.

'It's been some battle,' Mex muttered as they drew close to the end of Main Street.

There was still plenty of shooting, some directed at the stone building where the raiders were holed up and a good deal coming out of the building itself. It was one of only a few stone-built buildings in town and it had been a bank.

Jordan and Mex and Stevenoak crouched and edged their way forward to where soldiers were shooting from the cover of overturned wagons and anything they could drag between them and the building.

A captain loomed up from behind another building. 'Get back!' he ordered. 'This is as far as you can go!'

'You Captain Taylor?' Jordan asked him.

'Who wants to know?'

'I'm Jordan. Been talking to your sergeant. Is Coulter in there, Captain?'

'He's in there all right. Been shouting and swearing and shooting. Killed two of my men. Coulter's a madman, you know that?' Captain Taylor seemed a little on edge like this was his first taste of battle.

146

'Should know Coulter's mad as hell,' Jordan said. 'We rode together in the recent war. Nearly died together a bunch of times.'

The captain paused to stroke his lean jaw. 'Heard of you, Jordan. McGill, that Pinkerton man who called us in, warned us about you. Thought you might be working for those rebel raiders.'

'Those rebel raiders killed my pa!' Jordan retorted angrily. 'You want Coulter out of there, I can bring him out. Might save the lives of a few of your men.'

Captain Taylor considered matters. 'You think you can talk him out?'

'I could try,' Jordan said. 'How many d'you reckon are in there?'

The captain rubbed his jaw again. 'Maybe six, maybe two. Hard to say.'

'Tell your men to hold their fire,' Jordan said.

'What d'you aim to do?' Mex muttered.

'Always good to talk . . . one way or the other,' Jordan laughed.

They edged forward with the captain until they were within good hailing distance of the stone building now pitted with bullet marks. Captain Taylor gave the order for his men to hold their fire. A gloomy silence draped itself over the scene. In the distance they could still hear the groans of the dying and shouts of the citizens fighting to extinguish the fires.

The sergeant crawled up and handed Jordan a megaphone. Jordan passed the megaphone to Mex and cupped his hands.

'You there, Coulter?' he shouted.

There was a deafening quiet in the besieged building.

Jordan cupped his hands again. 'Captain Coulter, this is your old sergeant Nat Jordan. Can you hear me?'

Another moment of silence. Then a voice through the darkness. 'Is that you, Sergeant Jordan, or just someone pretending to be you?' the voice demanded.

'I think you know the answer to that, Captain,' Jordan replied.

Another brief silence. 'What's your proposition, Sergeant?' the voice of Coulter came again.

'I'm here to talk,' Jordan said.

Another longer silence. 'You here to talk, you better come along in,' Coulter shouted.

Jordan rose slowly from behind the barrier. Captain Taylor grabbed his arm to restrain him. 'You can't go in there,' he said to Jordan but Jordan shook him off.

'I'm coming in,' he shouted.

'You come real slow,' Coulter replied. 'And don't bring any of those soldier boys with you. Tell them to keep back and hold their fire. You and me can have a little pow wow. Be like old times, eh?' He chuckled in a strange unnerving way.

Mex moved forward to stand beside Jordan. 'You can't go in there. It would be suicide. I heard you make a promise to Beth you wouldn't get yourself into any more trouble.'

Jordan turned to scan him briefly. 'This is unfinished business,' he said.

Mex stared at him for a moment. Then he nodded and drew back.

Jordan shouted again. 'OK, Captain, I'm coming in. You hold your fire and remember those glory days!'

Jordan rose and held up his arms. Nobody had said anything about unstrapping his gunbelt, so he still had the Colt at his hip.

It seemed a long walk to the stone building. No sound. There wasn't a flicker of light inside. It might have been

deep and blank for a thousand years. But then came a kind
of omen: from behind the smoke and the cloud the moon
suddenly broke through as though the eye of a pagan god
had pulled aside a blanket to watch the sad doings of half
crazy men.

As Jordan drew closer, the door creaked open and a low
voice said, 'Step inside real slow. We don't want any misun-
derstandings here, do we now?'

Jordan went inside and closed the door behind him. The
welcome moonlight slanted in through the windows and it
was like the inside of an ancient chapel on some distant
planet.

'You have guts, Sergeant. I always knew that. Lucky you
kept your leg that time. Otherwise we wouldn't be here.'

Jordan's eyes were adjusting to the light. Now he could
distinguish Coulter and saw he had a shooter trained on
him right between his eyes. Jordan glanced to left and right.
A man lay dying under a window. Two more bodies were
flung sideways in the grotesque postures of death.

'So, I got here just in time,' Jordan said. He could see the
glint of Coulter's grinning teeth in the moonlight.

'Just in time,' Coulter said. He cocked the pistol and held
it steady on Jordan's face. 'I guess you knew we were riding
in on the town,' he said. 'I thought maybe Rig had shot you
down after that little chat we had by the old-timer's place.
But it seems you got the drop on him.' He paused. 'That
goof McGill sent a wire through to the army in Kansas City.
One of my men in the telegraph office intercepted the
message. So we were set to punish him.' He paused to
consider. 'Lucky for him you shot him before he choked his
life out at the end of that rope. I knew that was you, Jordan.
That's your style. You're a damned sight too soft for this
world.'

'That's as maybe,' Jordan said.

149

'Sure,' Coulter agreed. 'The soft and the damned,' he concluded. He nodded slowly to himself. 'We've travelled a long road together, Sergeant Jordan, you know that?' He gestured with the revolver but still kept it trained on Jordan's head.

'It has been long,' Jordan conceded.

'And now that long and winding road has come to an end,' Coulter said. He moved the revolver down to cover Jordan's heart. 'You want to make a play for that gun on your hip I could blast the hell out of you where you stand, you know that?'

Jordan nodded and his mouth felt like it was full of sand. 'I know that, Captain,' he said.

'And I guess you'd deserve it, Sergeant,' Coulter drawled. There was another silence. Jordan could have taken a quick step forward and attempted to sweep the Colt aside, but he made no move.

'But I don't aim to do that,' Coulter said. 'Of course, I could ask you to make another suggestion. You could make a break for it with me. We could blast out together and kill a few more of those moron soldiers before they cut us down, or maybe try to get away through the back of the building, but I don't aim to do that either. I'm going to ask a special favour of you, Sergeant, as one soldier to another. Kind of bond of brotherhood.'

Jordan felt his heart shrink to a stone but he made no move.

Coulter breathed in deeply. 'You know what that special favour is, Sergeant?'

Jordan kept himself as still as the stone he felt he had become and said nothing.

Coulter was grinning like a death mask in the moonlight. 'It seems I lost this last battle,' he said. 'But I'm a soldier, Jordan, and I don't aim to give myself up to those Yankee fools.' The grin seemed to get wider and more deathlike. 'What I'm going to do is, lay this shooter aside. And what you do is draw that Colt you got on your hip and shoot me right between the eyes. Matter of honour between soldiers, like Brutus falling on his sword.' He paused. 'Can you do that, Jordan?'

Jordan said nothing and made no move.

Coulter gave a faint sigh. 'You could do it as a matter of honour between soldiers and buddies,' he said. 'But, if you want some motivation, think of your pa swinging in that ranch house and remember it was me who gave the order.' He lowered the Colt until it was almost on the floor.

The muscles in Jordan's jaw tensed but he still said nothing.

Coulter nodded slowly. 'See what I've done, Sergeant. See what I've done. I've lowered my gun. All you've got to do is draw that Colt on your hip, cock it, put it to my head and fire. That way you come out of this with honour. Those bastards out there will give you a medal. You walk away smelling of roses.'

Now Jordan stirred and spoke. 'You know I can't do that, Captain,' he said quietly. 'Best thing you can do is give yourself up and face your trial like a man.'

'Like a man, eh!' Coulter jeered.

Jordan nodded. 'It takes a man to recognize he's done wrong and take the rap. That's the only thing you can do. Give yourself up and face the music.'

Coulter started to laugh. 'Quite the poet, aren't we?' he said.

He raised the gun and pointed it straight at Jordan again. 'Goodnight, Sergeant,' he said.

But he turned the gun and took it between his teeth. There was a pulpy explosion of blood and brains and Coulter was dead.

151

As Jordan staggered out of the building, Mex came rushing towards him with a drawn Colt. Jordan pushed on past him and stood with his knees trembling, facing the moon.

The moon looked bigger and brighter than he had ever seen it before and he breathed in its silver beauty.

CHAPTER TWELVE

Old Man Armitage had the newspaper spread on the table before him. When he had taken his breakfast he would go out and instruct his men what to do. Then he would retire for a well-earned rest in the rocking-chair on the porch. He would spread the paper, which was more than a week old, and study it through his newly acquired spectacles – the ones he had gotten in Kansas City a few weeks back. It didn't matter that the paper was old. Armitage had a taste for news, but he was more interested in history, especially the history of the recent rebellion and how it had been crushed by the army with a little help from Nathaniel Jordan, Mex and Beth Armitage. Especially Beth Armitage, his daughter.

'Well, I'll be darned tootin,' he chuckled as Beth came out onto the porch.

He looked up at her and shaded his eyes. There was a nip in the air which he recognized as the first touch of fall, a season he enjoyed but which didn't last long enough.

'When's that good-for-nothing Nat Jordan coming over?' he sang out in a high cracked tone.

Beth was smiling. There was no more smut or signs of scorching on her skin and she looked like some kind of delicious fruit, an apple maybe or a peach of some kind. That girl Beth sure had a neat complexion these days.

Beth looked away from her father and saw what she was

waiting to see, a man riding towards the Armitage spread.

'Here's Nat,' she said.

Armitage looked up quickly and peered in the direction of the approaching rider. The paper slid down from his knees and on to the plank floor. 'Well don't stand there, girl. Welcome him in. That man's a hero. It says so here.' He looked round for the paper and made a grab at it. 'Pick that paper up for me, will you, for the sake of truth?'

But Beth was already on the edge of the veranda. She didn't wave or call out. That wasn't her style. She just stood there waiting and watching with her hands clasped across her breast as Jordan approached.

He, too, was looking a deal more sprightly, you could say well scrubbed, as he guided Regius up to the house. Had a haircut too, Beth noticed when he raised his Stetson to her. Cary had taken the scissors and trimmed him down. Beth felt a twinge of jealousy; she wasn't quite sure she approved of Cary and those scissors.

She reached up and touched Jordan on the waist. Jordan looked down at her and saw the glint of fire in her eyes. Something turned over inside him and he knew what he had come for.

'Well, my boy!' Mr Armitage sang out. 'So you came at last. How's your sister and your ma? Are they drifting over for supper tonight?'

Jordan nodded. 'They're coming over later with the buckboard.'

'How's your ma doing?'

'Ma's OK,' Jordan said. 'I would say she's almost back to normal, got used to living in the house again after my pa's death.'

'He was a good man,' Armitage mused, 'and a good friend to me too.' He scrabbled about on the boards and scooped up the newspaper. 'Did you see this account of what happened in Redsville?'

Jordan nodded. 'I saw it. Those newspaper men know how to make a story.' He looked at Beth and cocked one eyebrow.

'Darn tootin they do,' Armitage agreed. 'But there's no exaggerating here. This time it's the truth. Your old man would be right proud of you.'

Jordan wasn't sure of that. But he would never know. He swung his leg over Regius and landed on the ground. Beth saw the old bounce in his step and felt the blood stirring in her veins.

'See you later,' Jordan said to her quietly.

'Sure thing,' Beth's father sang out. 'See you all come at suppertime. You've got to give me the inside story so I can write it up and paste it in my album alongside this newspaper account . . . for the grandchildren.' He gave Jordan a broad wink.

Mrs Armitage came out onto the veranda. 'What are you prattling on about, you old fool?' she said to her husband.

Armitage turned to her with a wide grin that showed the gaps between his teeth. 'Just telling these young folk I want to hear the full story from their own lips,' he said.

'Well, you old scallywag, you'd best leave them alone. Nat doesn't like talking about that. You know, he's modest. Doesn't like to boast like you.'

'That so?' he said. He turned to look at the young folk but they had vanished completely.

Jordan was making Regius comfortable in the stable when Mex rode in from repairing the fence line.

'Hi there,' he said

Mex gave him a casual salute and looked faintly hangdog. 'Thought you should know, I'm thinking of going back to Mexico.'

Jordan nodded but showed no surprise.

'You got business back there?' he said.

'Could have,' Mex said evasively.

Jordan was looking pensive. 'A man has to make up his own mind. There's plenty to do around here if a man wanted to stay.'

Mex nodded and took the saddle off his horse. He went out and left Jordan to turn things over in his mind.

When Jordan looked up again he saw Beth watching him from the doorway. 'Mex has to stay,' she said. 'We can't let him go like that, not after what we've been through together.'

Jordan straightened up and had that strange uneasy feeling inside again. 'Tell you something,' he said, 'Mex has to make his own way. He's a good man. Nobody could doubt that after what happened down at Redsville.'

They stood looking at one another and he saw the challenge in her eyes. 'We have to talk about this,' she said.

He didn't ask what. He just nodded.

'I mean, what happened, why you broke your promise,' she said. 'We never talked it through.'

He nodded again.

'Why you walked in on Coulter like that after you'd told me you wouldn't put yourself in danger.'

Jordan breathed in slowly. 'You know I had to make that promise, Beth. You're such a wild woman you might have wanted to come into that building with me, and I couldn't have that.'

She was smiling ruefully. 'You don't want to talk about Coulter, do you?' she said.

'It's tough,' he admitted. 'A man you've fought with back to back, a man who kills your pa, a man who leads a rebellion. It's tough.'

'I know,' she agreed. 'I have to ask you something. When

156

you went into that building they thought you were crazy. Did you expect to come out alive?'

Jordan knitted his brows and tried to think. 'Tell you the truth, I didn't know what to think. I knew Coulter wouldn't give himself up, not to me, not to any man. I figured I had to kill him, or he would kill me. Didn't expect it, the way things turned out. I should have done, I guess. Should have realized Coulter was so fanatical nothing would stop him. So in a way I made him do what he did.' He looked away and then back again. He saw the softening in her eyes.

'Nat Jordan,' she said, 'I might have lost you, but you did a brave thing. If they give you some kind of medal, you deserve it.'

Jordan looked faintly surprised and felt deeply relieved. They came together and stayed together, and time seemed to lose its meaning.

Up at the house Stevenoak was waiting. He wanted to talk to Jordan. Said he wanted to get things straight about the events of that *terrible* night. Though Jordan considered the sheriff a blabbermouth who talked more than he acted, he decided to give him his say.

They sat out on the porch together and Stevenoak produced a cob pipe that he proceeded to smoke, looking like an ancient prophet.

'I've been thinking things over,' he said, 'and I believe I owe you an apology.'

'Forget it,' Jordan said. 'That's all water under the bridge.'

Stevenoak nodded sagely. 'That's as maybe and I thank you for it, but I have to say there was a time I really thought you were part of that Quantrill bunch. The whole situation was difficult to read what with you knowing Coulter in the war and that.'

157

He puffed at his outsized pipe for a time and a grin crept over his face.

'But by Jehosophat, we smoked them out, didn't we, Nat?'

'We got a little help from the army,' Jordan conceded.

Stevenoak frowned at his pipe. 'Pity about that Pinkerton man, McGill. It was the guy in the telegraph office betrayed him, but he couldn't have known what those Quantrills would do to him.'

Jordan nodded. He could still see the writhing figure of McGill the moment before he took the shot that killed him. That was a lucky shot but it had started the whole shooting match!

Stevenoak smoked on in contentment for a while. 'Pity about that guy they called Preacher Man. Friend of yours, I hear.' He gave Jordan and enquiring look, but Jordan didn't respond. He had heard that they found Preacher Man's body still clutching his charred but precious fiddle.

Not much left of the Washington or several other properties along Main Street.

'That was something of a massacre,' Stevenoak reflected. 'Fifteen men killed, five soldiers and ten of those so-called Quantrills.' He stretched out his hand like he was reviewing the corpses. 'Ten Quantrill stiffs lined up on the sidewalk along Main Street. Those rebels didn't look too pretty either, I can tell you, 'specially Coulter. They covered what was left of his face with an old gunny sack.' He removed his pipe and reflected again. 'But I don't have to tell you that. You saw the whole thing. We were set to rush the place, you know, but you got in there first.'

He closed his eyes and the perfumed smoke from his pipe rose in a cloud into the still air.

'Now, what's your next move, Nat? What do you aim to do?'

158

He turned to look at Jordan. But Jordan had moved away. He was on the edge of the porch looking way off into the twilight.

At supper that night there was great rejoicing in the Armitage place. Beth's mother had cooked up a fine supper, and they were all seated at the long table with Mr Armitage at the head and Nat Jordan at the other end with Beth beside him. Ranged along the table were Jordan's mother, more herself again, and Cary, his sister, looking pert and important. Jordan's other sisters had returned home a few days before. And Mex, of course: he was sitting there on Jordan's right looking slightly out of place.

There was a quiet air of festivity round the table as both families celebrated the hunter's return from the field. Nobody expected much more than good wholesome food and home-brewed beer until Jordan banged on the table with his mug and rose to speak.

Jordan wasn't good at speechmaking but he knew what he wanted to say. Most of the women noticed that he and Beth were holding hands and they soon learned why. The hunter had returned from the field and he intended to settle down and stay. Jordan and Beth had decided to get married in the spring when the whole country was bursting into leaf.

There was the usual burst of applause from round the table, and then Mr Armitage decided to say a few words. He rambled on joyfully for twenty minutes or so until his wife tugged at his sleeve and stage-whispered in his ear. 'Sit down, you old fool, before you make yourself look like an idiot.'

It made no difference to Armitage. He laughed and went on all the same.

*

They got married in April and, though he wasn't a talking *hombre* Mex acted as best man. In the course of time, the two spreads came together and became one with Jordan in control and Beth a close second. Mex went down to Mexico and returned shortly after with a girl called Rosetta. He stayed on as top waddy and the ranch too began to expand and grow. But growth doesn't come without pain and that's another story.